"Don't try to sugarcoat the facts, Sebastian. We had a one-night stand!"

"Stop it, Lily!"

"Why, am I speaking the truth too plainly?"

"It's not the truth and you know it."

"No?" A lone tear trembled on her lashes.

"You want to know something?" he muttered. "I wish we could have met under different circumstances. Perhaps if we had…"

"We might have fallen in love? I don't think so, Sebastian. Love doesn't come calling only when it's convenient. Please let me go. I can't bear your being kind to me like this."

"It's not kindness. God help me, I want you, Lily. More than ever. And I think you want me, too."

CATHERINE SPENCER, once an English teacher, fell into writing through eavesdropping on a conversation about Harlequin romances. Within two months she changed careers and sold her first book to Harlequin in 1984. She moved to Canada from England more than thirty years ago and lives in Vancouver. She is married to a Canadian and has four grown children—two daughters and two sons—plus three dogs and a cat. In her spare time she plays the piano, collects antiques and grows tropical shrubs.

Books by Catherine Spencer

HARLEQUIN PRESENTS®

Don't miss any of our special offers. Write to us at the following address for information on our newest releases.

Harlequin Reader Service
U.S.: 3010 Walden Ave., P.O. Box 1325, Buffalo, NY 14269
Canadian: P.O. Box 609, Fort Erie, Ont. L2A 5X3

Catherine Spencer

MISTRESS ON HIS TERMS

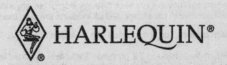

HARLEQUIN®

TORONTO • NEW YORK • LONDON
AMSTERDAM • PARIS • SYDNEY • HAMBURG
STOCKHOLM • ATHENS • TOKYO • MILAN • MADRID
PRAGUE • WARSAW • BUDAPEST • AUCKLAND

ISBN 0-373-12197-0

MISTRESS ON HIS TERMS

First North American Publication 2001.

Copyright © 2001 by Kathy Garner.

Visit us at www.eHarlequin.com

Printed in U.S.A.

CHAPTER ONE

"I'LL be waiting by the baggage claim carousel," Hugo Preston had told her, when they'd spoken by phone the night before. "You'll know me by my gray hair and the bouquet of roses I'll have brought for you—red roses, because tomorrow's a red-letter day for me. I'm counting the hours until we meet, Lily."

But the other passengers had already collected their belongings and gone, leaving Lily standing alone with her two suitcases and carry-on bags stowed in a luggage cart. Although there'd been a number of older men with gray hair waiting to meet the Vancouver flight when it landed on time in Toronto, none had been carrying roses, nor had any come forward to identify himself as her biological father.

Caught between a sense of letdown and resentment—so much for his anxiety to connect with the daughter he'd always known about but never met!—Lily took out the map tucked in the side pocket of her purse.

Stentonbridge, the small town where Hugo maintained a year-round residence, lay some hundred and fifty miles northeast of Toronto, so she supposed that, because of the heavy rains in the area, it was conceivable that the drive had taken longer than he'd expected.

But then, another scenario rose up to haunt her. What if, even as she stood there silently berating him for his apparent parental disregard, a car crushed beyond recognition was being hauled out of a ravine, and the man she'd

5

come so far to meet lay covered by a sheet in an ambulance bound for the nearest morgue?

Refusing to allow the thought to take root, she stuffed the map back into her bag. Tragedy like that didn't strike twice in a row; it was the terrible exception, not the rule. There was some other perfectly plausible reason for Hugo's tardiness, and quite possibly a message explaining it waiting to be picked up at the airline information desk. If not, he'd given her a number where he could be reached.

Wheeling around, she scanned the arrivals terminal again. A lull between incoming flights left the immediate area relatively uncrowded. Apart from a family of four trying to pack a baby as well as their overflowing bags into one cart, a group of students gathered around their tour leader, and a man forging a purposeful path between the lot of them, she remained in conspicuous isolation.

The man was imposingly tall and the crowd, small though it was, fell back to allow him passage in much the same way, Lily thought with dry amusement, that Moses might have parted the Red Sea. Craning her neck, she peered past him, searching for the familiar Air Canada logo.

He, however, appeared determined not only to obstruct her view but also to occupy the one spot in the whole vast place to which she'd laid claim. In fact, the way he was zeroing in on her, he might have intended running her clean into the ground.

"You're looking for me," he announced tersely, coming to a stop so close that she had to tilt her head back to look into his face and the most arrestingly cold blue eyes she'd ever seen.

But *gray-haired, elderly and kindly* hardly fit his description. "Oh, no, I'm not!" she informed him with equal brevity and attempted to push past him.

He had a hold of her buggy, though, and it wasn't going anywhere without his permission. "You're Lily Talbot," he said, and it occurred to Lily that any other man would have couched the words as a question. But this modern-day Moses wasn't subject to the limitations of the rest of humanity. Preferential treatment from on high had blessed him with special powers. No doubt he could have told her what brand of toothpaste she used, if she'd been of a mind to inquire!

Instead she said stiffly, "More to the point, who are you?"

"Sebastian Caine."

He introduced himself as if the mere mention of his name should be enough to start bells of recognition clanging in the mind of even the most dim-witted person. Not about to cater to such a monumental ego, Lily said, "How nice!" and gave her buggy a determined shove. "Unhand my cart, please. I'd like to make a phone call and find out what happened to the person I'm supposed to meet."

"No need," he said, not budging an inch. "I'm your chauffeur."

Clearly he no more relished the idea of driving her to Stentonbridge than she did. "Oh, I don't think so," she said. "I don't climb into cars with strange men."

A flicker of what might have been a smile twitched the corners of his mouth before he wrestled it back into its former severe line. "You haven't known me long enough to label me 'strange,' Miss Talbot."

"It's 'Ms.,'" she said. "And regardless of whatever label you care to hang around your neck, I'm not getting into a car with you. I'll wait until Mr. Preston gets here."

"Hugo isn't coming."

She'd been afraid of that. "Why not?"

"Because I persuaded him to stay at home."

"And he always does as you tell him, does he?"

"Not as often as he should," Sebastian Caine said bitterly. "If he did, you wouldn't be here now and I wouldn't be wasting my time carrying on this inane conversation. Let go of the damned luggage cart, for pity's sake! I'm not about to abscond with it—or you, come to that. But I would like to load up and be out of here before the rush hour gets any worse."

He'd referred to Hugo by his first name without any prompting from her. He'd known who she was. He wore a look of unimpeachable propriety. His clothes, his watch, even his haircut were expensive, and he no more resembled a kidnapper than she did a call girl. But appearances could be deceiving, as she'd learned to her considerable cost. "I'm not going anywhere with you until I've verified your identity with my father," she said.

He stiffened and a grimace of aversion rolled over his face, as if her referring to Hugo as her father was an affront to decent society. Lips compressed in annoyance, he produced a cell phone from the inside pocket of his jacket, punched in a two-digit code and thrust the instrument at her. "Be my guest."

She accepted it warily, still not entirely sure she ought to trust him. But a glance at the illuminated screen showed Hugo's name and number.

"Will you for pity's sake hit Send and get on with it," Sebastian Caine snapped, noting her reluctance. "It's a phone, not a bomb. It won't explode in your hand."

Hugo answered on the third ring. "I'm so glad you called, Lily," he said. "There's been a slight change in plan—an old back injury's flared up to give me grief, so my stepson Sebastian's meeting your flight and driving you up here. He's about six foot three, dark haired, good-looking so the women tell me, and hard to miss even in a crowd.''

Add rude, arrogant and condescending, and the description would be complete, Lily thought. "We've met,'' she said, glaring at Sebastian Caine and itching to wipe the smug expression off his face. "He's standing in front of me, even as we speak.'' *Not to mention practically stealing the air I breathe!*

"Excellent! Ask him if we should hold dinner for you.''

She did so, and could have been forgiven for thinking, from the way Sebastian commandeered the phone and hunched one shoulder away from her, that his answer conveyed information pertinent to national security. His voice carried loud and clear, though, as he said, "Hugo? Better not wait dinner for us. This afternoon's meeting ran late and I've got one more call to make before I head back.''

Whatever Hugo replied had Sebastian casting her another of his disapproving looks. "I suppose so, if you like that sort of thing,'' he eventually said, "but I can't say I see any startling family resemblance. She could be anybody from anywhere.''

He made it sound as if she were something unwholesome he'd scraped off the sidewalk! If it weren't that she had no more sense of direction than a drunken field mouse, she'd have dearly loved to rent her own car and tell him to stick his offer to drive her where it would lodge most uncomfortably. Instead she swallowed her pride and allowed him to hustle her and her baggage out to the parking area.

Practically sprinting to keep up with him as he plowed his way to where he'd left his car, she asked, "How long will it take to drive to Stentonbridge?''

"Normally around three hours. Today, because of the weather and delays, more like four or five."

To say he sounded ticked off gave grim new meaning to the word understatement. "I'm sorry you've been inconvenienced on my account. I'd have been just as happy to take a train or bus."

"None run from here to Stentonbridge and even if one did, Hugo wouldn't hear of it." His voice took on a derisive edge. "You're the long-lost daughter returning to the fold, and he wants you welcomed in style."

"It's rather obvious you don't share his enthusiasm."

He spared her a brief, dismissive glance. "Why should I? Even if you're who you claim you are—"

"There's no *even if* about it," she said. "I have documented proof."

"Which has yet to be verified as authentic." He swung the luggage cart to a halt behind a sports car as long, dark and sleekly handsome as its owner, popped open the trunk and started piling her bags inside. "You want any of this stuff in the front with you?"

"No."

"Then since the door's unlocked, climb in and get settled. I'm in a hurry."

"Well, silly me!" she said sweetly. "Here I thought you were merely in training for a decathlon!"

He raised one winged brow and cast her a look that might have turned a more prudent woman to stone. "Don't push your luck, Ms. Talbot. You've already tried my patience to the limit."

"And how have I done that, Sebastian?"

His pinched nostrils told her exactly what he thought of such untoward familiarity. "You're here, aren't you?" he said. "Isn't that enough?"

"But I'm not here to see *you*. In fact, crushing though

it might be for you to hear this, I didn't even know of your existence until ten minutes ago.''

''You raise an interesting question nonetheless,'' he said, slamming closed the trunk and ushering her into the passenger seat with more haste than gallantry before sliding his rangy frame behind the steering wheel. ''Why, after all this time, do you want to see Hugo?''

''He's my father. What better reason is there?''

''But why now? If you're telling the truth, he's been your father all your life.''

''I didn't know that until recently.''

''Precisely my point, Ms. Talbot. You've managed without him for the better part of twenty-six years. You're well past the point where you need a guardian. There's no emotional tie between you. So what's the real reason you're suddenly sniffing around?''

He made her sound like an ill-bred bloodhound. ''It's highly personal and not something I choose to share with a total stranger.''

''There are no secrets between Hugo and me.''

''Apparently there are,'' she said smugly. ''Judging by your reaction to my sudden appearance, he never confided to you that he had a daughter waiting in the wings.''

''Maybe,'' Sebastian replied, giving back as good as he got, ''because he never missed you. The daughter he *does* know and love more than compensated for your absence.''

''I have a...sister?'' The concept struck a strangely unsettling, though not unpleasant note. She had been an only child who'd always wanted to be part of a big family, but there hadn't even been cousins she could be close to. No aunts or uncles, and no grandparents. Just her mother and the man she'd known as her father. ''We don't need anyone else,'' he'd often said. ''The three of us have each other.''

Three, that was, until the September day ten months before, when a police officer showed up at her door and told her her parents were among the fatalities of a multivehicle accident on a foggy highway in North Carolina.

"Half sister," Sebastian Caine said. "Natalie is Hugo's child by his second marriage to my mother."

"So what does that make you and me?" she asked, aiming to introduce a more cordial tone to the conversation. "Half stepbrother and sister?"

He cut her off in a voice as cold and sharp as the blade of an ax. "It makes us nothing."

"Well, praise heaven!" she replied, stung.

"Indeed."

They'd cleared the airport by then and joined the stream of traffic headed through the pouring rain for downtown Toronto. He was probably a very skilled driver, but the memory of her parents as they'd looked when she'd gone to make a positive identification remained too fresh in her mind, and the way Sebastian Caine zipped around slower vehicles left her bracing herself for disaster.

"Keep pumping an imaginary brake like that, and you'll wind up putting your foot through the floor," he observed, zooming up behind another car with what struck her as cavalier disregard for safety.

"I don't fancy ending up in someone else's trunk, that's all."

He sort of smiled. At least, she supposed that was what the movement of his lips amounted to. "Do I make you nervous, Ms. Talbot?"

She closed her eyes as he changed lanes and zipped past a moving truck. "Yes."

"Then you're wiser than I expected."

Her eyes flew open again. "What's that supposed to mean?"

"It means I don't trust you or your motives. It means I'll be watching every move you make while you're here. Put a foot wrong, and I'll be all over you."

"How exciting. Be still my heart!"

"I'm serious."

"I can see that you are. What puzzles me is why I'm such a threat to your peace of mind. I assure you I don't plan to run off with the family silver or murder people in their beds. I have questions that only Hugo Preston can answer, that's all."

"You didn't have to come halfway across the country for that. The telephone was invented a long time ago."

"I'm curious to meet my father face-to-face."

"I just bet you are!" he sneered.

She shrugged. "So sue me."

"Give me reason to, and I will."

She stared at him, unable to fathom his hostility, but his expression gave nothing away and she wasn't about to beg for an explanation. "I'm afraid you're in for a terrible disappointment," she said instead. "I have no hidden agenda in coming here."

His mouth tightened.

"There's nothing unnatural in a person wanting to meet her biological parent."

He glanced in the rearview mirror, stepped on the accelerator and raced past a stretch limo. Prickles of sweat broke out along her spine as he took an off-ramp at alarming speed.

Thrusting both palms flat against the dashboard, she asked, "How many auto accidents have you had?"

The question was ill-advised, to say the least. He speared her with a chilly sideways glare, which glimmered with evil amusement. "None. But there's a first time for everything."

"Well, if it's all the same to you, I'd prefer you postpone the premiere performance until I'm not your passenger."

"Your preferences don't rank high on my list of priorities, Ms. Talbot. In fact, it's safe to say they don't register at all. As for your perceived sense of danger, let me assure you I don't intend risking either life or limb on your account."

They'd turned onto a street lined with elegant town houses by then. Braking to a stop next to a van, he shifted into reverse and began backing into a parking space so tight, it invited disaster. She opened her mouth to tell him so, then snapped it closed again as, without a moment's hesitation or a single false move, he angled the car into place and brought it to rest parallel to the curb.

He reached behind her seat, leaning close enough that she got a pleasant whiff of his aftershave, and hauled out a briefcase. "Wait here," he ordered, climbing out of the car. "I won't be long."

Lily watched as he loped across the street and up the steps to a door three houses down. Before he had the chance to ring the bell, a woman appeared. She was very pleased to see him, if the smile and hug she bestowed were anything to go by, and she was also very pregnant. He slung an arm around her shoulders and the two of them disappeared inside the house.

Ten minutes passed, then twenty. The clouds, which had been dense enough to start with, grew even darker. Not long after, a light came on at an upstairs window of the house into which Sebastian Caine had disappeared.

"Oh, fine thing!" Lily muttered resentfully. "I'm left

cooling my heels in here while he has an assignation with his mistress. No wonder he told Hugo not to hold dinner!''

She twisted around and craned her neck, searching the narrow area behind the two front seats in the hope of finding something to wile away the time—a newspaper or magazine, even a map of the area. But the only item of interest was Sebastian's passport lying open and facedown on the floor.

She prided herself on being an essentially decent person, the kind who returned her library books on time, held open doors for the elderly, and told little white lies only when absolutely necessary. She definitely did not consider herself to be the sort who snooped through other people's medicine cabinets or read their mail. But that darned passport drew her like a magnet and before the full import of what she was doing could properly register, she found herself picking it up and sneaking a look inside.

In line with those of most other people she knew, her own passport picture made her look as if she belonged on North America's *Ten Most Wanted* list, but Sebastian Andrew Caine might have commissioned a portrait photographer to produce his. His face stared back at her in all its direct-gazed, firm-jawed glory.

He'd been blessed with impeccable cheekbones, thick black hair, eyelashes to draw the envy of every woman alive and a disarming cleft in his chin. On top of that, as she knew from firsthand observation, he stood well over six feet and probably sent his tailor into raptures over his trim, perfectly proportioned physique.

Too bad he'd been at the end of the receiving line when God dispensed charm!

Though now a Canadian citizen, he'd been born in Harrisburg, Pennsylvania, on April 23, thirty-four years ago. He traveled often and mostly to exotic places like Turkey, Russia, The Far East, Morocco and Greece.

She thumbed through the pages. His most recent port of call had been Cairo; his most far-flung Rarotonga. He'd visited Rio de Janeiro twice in the last three years and the southern Baja four times. What with jaunts all over the world and house calls to his current ladylove, it was a wonder he found time to work!

Annoyed at being kept waiting, Lily slapped the passport closed and turned to glare across the street at the house he'd entered, only to find her view blocked by Sebastian Caine's tall figure. Completely unmindful of the rain pelting down, he stood beside her window, glaring right back at her.

At the realization that she'd been caught blatantly prying into something that was absolutely none of her business, her whole body blushed, starting at her toes and spreading in waves until the blood suffused her face and left it burning. Even her throat and eyeballs felt parched. She could neither swallow nor blink. She simply sat in paralyzed horror and prayed he was a mirage created by the rain weaving patterns down the glass.

At best, it was an unlikely alternative and one he soon disabused her of by striding around the back of the car and wrenching open the driver's door.

Of course, there was no justifying what she'd been caught doing. Still, she felt compelled to try. "It was lying on the floor," she blustered, the minute he climbed into the car.

He didn't speak. He didn't have to. His raised eyebrows told her plainly enough what he thought of *that* as an excuse.

"So I picked it up. A passport's not something to be left lying around, you know."

He leaned back in his seat and continued his frigid, unblinking regard.

Self-preservation told her she was merely digging herself in deeper with every word and that her best bet was to keep quiet. But his silence, charged with unspoken accusation as it was, unnerved her. "I mean, it could just as easily have fallen out on the road without your noticing, and I'm sure you know what a hassle it is trying to get a replacement.... Particularly if you needed to travel overseas in a hurry... Not to mention the ramifications of some underworld figure getting hold of it and putting it to criminal use...and...well..."

"Are you quite done?" he asked, when she finally ran out of steam.

She looked down, realized she was still clutching the passport and hurriedly dropped it into his lap. "Yes."

"Thank God!"

He tossed the passport over his shoulder, and eased the car out of its parking spot. The rush hour was in full swing by then, which made it a bit easier for her to tolerate his aloof silence since she had no wish to distract him from the job of negotiating the heavy traffic. But when the city limits lay far behind them and the only sound to break the twilight hush was the frenzied swipe of the windshield wipers, she decided they'd both sulked long enough.

"I'm afraid," she said, slewing a glance at him, "that we got off to a rocky start and I'd like to apologize for my part in that."

His shrug of acknowledgment could hardly be construed as encouraging.

Still, she persevered. "I really don't make a habit of going through other people's private possessions, you know. But you were gone longer than you led me to expect and I was just looking for something to read."

He favored her with a scathing glance. "In that case, I suppose I should count myself lucky that you stopped with my passport. There must be at least a dozen legal files back there, which would have provided you with much juicier entertainment and after you'd read your fill, you could have blackmailed me for breaching lawyer-client confidentiality."

"I didn't know you're a lawyer."

"And I didn't know you're a meddlesome busybody, so that makes us even."

She shifted in her seat, the better to observe him. He really was quite outstandingly good-looking. "Why are you so determined to dislike me, Sebastian?"

"I have no feelings toward you, one way or the other, Ms. Talbot. I already told you, you're an inconvenience, but I'll get over that as soon as I've deposited you on Hugo's doorstep." He punctuated his statement with a telling pause before continuing, "Provided you don't hurt him or anyone else I care about."

"It's obvious you think I'll do exactly that."

He swung his head and pinioned her in his cold blue stare, and she almost cringed at the expression she saw in their depths. "Let's just say that, in my experience, the apple seldom falls far from the tree."

She stared at him, more perplexed by the second. "Meaning?"

"Meaning if you're anything like your mother—!"

But then, as if he'd given away more than he intended, he clamped his mouth shut and returned his attention to the road.

Lily, though, wasn't so inclined to let the subject drop. "What do you know about my mother?"

"More than I care to."

"Because of things Hugo's told you?"

"Hugo had no contact with her for more than twenty-six years."

"Exactly! Which make his opinions less than reliable."

"Then for once we're in agreement." He flicked on the right turn indicator and slowed the car as they approached the neon-lit entrance to a restaurant set back about fifty yards from the road. "On which fortuitous note, I propose we stop for something to eat. Stentonbridge is still a good two hours' drive away."

Part of her wanted to tell him she was more interested in having him explain his cryptic remarks than she was in food. But another, more cautious part urged her not to pursue the topic. That he knew more than he was telling was plain enough, but although she'd come here looking for answers, she didn't want them from him. Whether or not he'd admit it, there was too much anger seething beneath his surface, and she didn't relish the idea of it bursting loose on some dark country road miles from anywhere.

She'd waited this long to find out the truth. She could wait a few hours longer.

She wasn't what he'd anticipated. Watching her covertly as she studied the menu, he had trouble reconciling the woman sitting opposite him in the booth with his expectations of a vulgar, money-grubbing fortune hunter. He'd been prepared for flashy good looks, provocative necklines, big hair, fake fingernails and too much cheap jewelry. They fit the image. Lily Talbot did not.

Oh, he supposed she was pretty enough, in an ordinary sort of way. More than pretty, some might say. But the cheapness wasn't there, no matter how hard he searched for it. She had narrow, elegant feet. Her hands were delicate, the nails well-cared for and buffed to a soft shine.

Her features were small and regular. Patrician, almost. Her
dark brown hair lay smooth and shining against her cheek.
She looked out at the world from wide, candid eyes and
she smiled a lot. Her mouth was permanently upturned at
the corners, her lips soft and full.

Apart from a watch, her only other jewelry was a pair
of small gold earrings. She wore a blue denim skirt, which
came to just below her knees, a short-sleeved white blouse
buttoned to a vee at the front and sandals. Her legs were
bare and, he hadn't been able to help noticing, extremely
long and shapely. Her skin was lightly tanned and she'd
painted her toenails pink. They reminded him of dainty
little shells.

Ticked off, he glowered at her, knowing Hugo would
love her, that he'd accept her immediately and not once
question her motives for suddenly wanting to make contact with him. But the fact remained that her mother's
betrayal, over a quarter of a century before, had nearly
killed him, and it was Sebastian's self-appointed job to
make sure the daughter didn't finish the job now.

Unaware of his scrutiny, she tapped her fingernail
against her front teeth and continued to peruse the menu.
She had lovely teeth, a lovely smile. "For Pete's sake, I
invited you here to eat, not spend the night," he practically barked. "Make up your mind what you want to order."

"I like looking at menus," she said, rewarding him
with a look of pained reproach from her big brown eyes.

"Then you must be a very slow reader. I could have
memorized the entire thing in half the time you're taking
to get through it."

"Well, I'm not like you."

Hell, no! She was pure woman, and the fact that he
couldn't stop taking inventory of her assets was beginning

to irk him more than a little! "In case it's slipped your mind, Hugo's been waiting a long time to meet you. If it's all the same to you, I'd as soon not prolong his agony."

She slapped the menu closed and leaned back in the booth. "I'll have a large order of fries and a vanilla milk shake."

"You took all this time to decide on a milkshake and fries?" he asked incredulously.

"With ketchup."

"If that's all you want, we could have stopped at a fast-food drive-in and saved ourselves some time."

She collected her bag and the sweater she'd heaped on the bench. "Okay. Let's go find one."

"Stay where you are!"

He must have raised his voice more than he realized because the next thing he knew, the waitress had come barging over to their booth to inquire, "Your boyfriend giving you trouble, honey?"

Lily Talbot exploded into warm, infectious laughter, as if the woman had said something hilariously amusing. "Heavens, he's not my boyfriend!"

"And I'm not giving her trouble."

The waitress eyed him darkly. "You'd better not be." She fished out her notepad and waited with pen poised. "So what'll you have?"

He relayed Lily's request and ordered a steak sandwich and coffee for himself. "I thought women like you existed on salad and tofu," he said, while they waited for their food.

"Women like me?" She regarded him pertly. "And what kind of woman is that, Sebastian?"

"Under thirty and in thrall to the latest trend, no matter how outlandish it might be."

"You don't know much about women, do you?"

Enough to know you're bad for my concentration, he could have told her.

She leaned forward and he couldn't help noticing the graceful curve of her breasts beneath her blouse. He even found himself wondering if she was wearing a bra. Damn her!

"Real women aren't slaves to fashion, Sebastian," she informed him, her tone suggesting she found him singularly lacking in intelligence. "We make up our own rules."

"What happens if your rules don't coincide with men's?"

"Then we compromise, the way we have since the beginning of time."

"Sounds to me like a convenient excuse to do whatever you want, whenever you want, and not be held accountable for your actions."

She looked at him pityingly. "Don't you know that if you always go looking for the worst in people, you'll eventually find it?"

She was either a complete innocent or a contemptible schemer, and until he determined which, he wasn't about to let down his guard. "I don't have to go looking, Ms. Talbot. I live by the credo *Give a person enough rope and she'll eventually hang herself.*" He paused meaningfully. "You'd do well to remember that."

CHAPTER TWO

LILY shook her head in bewilderment, floored by his unremitting hostility. "Well, so much for striking up pleasant dinner conversation!"

"I'm sorry if the truth offends you. We can change the subject if you like, and talk about the weather instead."

"I'd prefer not to talk to you at all. You've been nothing but disagreeable from the minute you set eyes on me and I'm tired of trying to figure out why. I'm beginning to suspect you don't have to have a reason because you're the kind who makes a career out of being miserable."

"At least we're not harboring any illusions about what each of us thinks of the other."

There was no getting past that steely reserve of his, no hint of humanity or warmth in his makeup. He might be handsome as sin on the outside, but inside he was as dry as the law books he probably considered riveting bedtime reading. "Oh, go soak your head!" she snapped.

He looked mildly astonished, as if he thought he had a corner on the insult market. "Now who's being offensive?"

"I am," she allowed, "because trying to be pleasant about *anything* is a lost cause with you, Sebastian Caine. You're fixated on being as insufferable as possible, whether or not you have just cause."

Their meal arrived then, so she poured a dollop of ketchup on her plate and stabbed a fork into her French fries.

"No need to take out your frustrations on your food, Ms. Talbot. That's not my heart you're impaling."

More's the pity! "Oh, shut up!" she said, wondering why she'd ever thought coming here was a good idea in the first place. Hugo Preston might have sounded eager to meet her, but he hadn't cared enough to pursue the connection until she'd approached him. Given her other troubles, she didn't need the aggravation of having his obnoxious stepson enter the mix! "Just shut up and eat, and let's get this whole miserable evening over with as soon as possible."

But it was not to be. When at last they were ready to leave, the waitress brought more than their bill. "Hope you folks aren't planning to go far tonight. Just got word of flash floods right through the area. Police are asking people to stay off the roads."

"Oh, brother, just what I need to make the day complete!" Sebastian threw down a fistful of money and glowered at Lily as if she were in cahoots with God and had personally orchestrated the storm. "Grab your stuff and let's get moving."

"But if the police are warning people to stay put—?"

He took her elbow and hustled her out to the porch. "We don't have a whole lot of choice, unless you want to spend the night here."

"Perish the thought!"

A small river was running through the parking lot, a fact Lily discovered when she inadvertently stepped in it and felt water splashing up past her ankles. Not that it really mattered; by the time she flung herself into the car, she was soaked to the skin all over.

Sebastian hadn't fared much better. Great patches of rain darkened the shoulders of his pale gray suit jacket, the cuffs of his trousers were dripping, and his hair, like hers, was plastered to his head.

Muttering words unfit to be repeated in decent company, he fired up the engine, started the windshield wipers slapping and inched the car over the rutted ground toward the road. Before they'd even cleared the parking lot, the side windows had misted over and the air was filled with the smell of wet clothes and warm damp skin. In fact, Lily was pretty sure she could see steam rising from her skirt.

To describe the driving conditions as poor didn't approach reality. In fact, they were ghastly. The road ahead resembled a dark tunnel into which they were hurtling with no clear idea of where it might curve to the right or left.

Fists clenched so tight her fingernails gouged the palms of her hands, Lily huddled in her seat and prayed they'd reach Stentonbridge without incident. But they'd covered only about forty miles of the remaining distance when Sebastian brought the car to a sudden, screeching halt.

There was no sign of human habitation; no lights in farmhouses, no illuminated storefronts, no street lamps. Nothing but the driving rain pounding on the car roof like urgent jungle drums, and the dark shapes of trees twisting in the wind.

"Why are we stopping here?" she said. "Or aren't I allowed to ask?"

And then she saw. Where earlier in the day there'd been a bridge over a ravine, there now was a torrent of muddy water cascading down the hillside and taking with it everything that stood in its path. Another twenty feet, and the car would have careened into empty space, then plunged into the swirling rapids.

"Precisely," Sebastian said, hearing her shocked gasp.

It was late July. High summer in that part of Ontario. Even the nights were warm. But suddenly she was freezingly cold and shivering so hard that her teeth rattled.

This was how it happened: one minute people were alive, with the blood flowing through their veins, and their minds full of plans for the next day, the next year…and then, in less time than it took to blink, it was all over. That's how it had been for her parents, and how it had almost been for her.

Tragedy wasn't selective in its choice of victims; it could strike twice.

She tried to breathe and could not. The air inside the car was too close, too drenched, and she was suffocating. With a strangled moan, she released the buckle of her seat belt and fumbled for the door handle.

Her lungs were bursting. She had to get out—out into the open air. With a mighty shove, she sent the door flying wide and half-fell, half-crawled from her seat. Never mind the rain pelting down, or the wind whipping wet strands of hair across her face. Anything was better than being locked in the close confines of that long, low-slung burgundy car, which all at once looked and felt too much like a mahogany coffin.

Blind with panic, she set off through the wild night with one thought uppermost in her mind: to find her way back to the brightly lit safety of the roadside café. She'd covered no more than a few feet, however, before she blundered full tilt into a solid wall of resistance and felt her arms pinioned in an iron hold.

"Have you lost your tiny mind?" Sebastian Caine bellowed, raising his voice above the din of the waterfall. "What the devil do you think you're doing?"

"We were almost killed!"

"And almost isn't good enough? You want to finish off the job?"

"I w-want..." But the irrational, superstitious terror that had propelled her out of the car and sent her stumbling away in the dark refused to translate into words. She tasted salt and was astonished to find tears mingling with the rain on her face. To her shame, a great ugly sob broke loose from her throat.

"Stop that!" he ordered. "Nothing's happened yet. At least have the decency to wait until real calamity strikes before you decide to fall apart." He gave her a little shake, but the hint of sympathy texturing his next remark showed he wasn't as blind to the cause of her distress as he'd first appeared. "Look, I appreciate that your parents' accident must still be pretty vivid in your mind, but letting your imagination run wild isn't helping. Get a grip, Lily, and go back to the car."

"I don't think I can," she wailed.

Even though the night was black as the inside of a cave, she sensed his frustration. "Then let me make it easy for you!"

Before she knew what was happening, he bent down, grabbed her behind her knees and flung her, firefighter-fashion, over his shoulder. Oblivious to her shriek of outrage or her hands clawing at his back, he marched back to the car and tossed her into the passenger seat as if she were a sack of potatoes.

"You've taxed my patience enough for one day," he informed her savagely, yanking her seat belt into place, "so don't even think about pulling another stunt like the last one, or you *will* wind up alone on the side of the road and let me tell you, it won't be an experience you'll want to talk about—always assuming, of course, that you survive the night." Then, as a further inducement to comply with his orders, "You do know, of course, that this whole area's swarming with cougars and snakes. And vampire bats."

He slammed her door, raced back to the driver's side and climbed in.

"You're lying," she said shakily. "Especially about the bats."

In the glow from the dashboard, his grin and the whites of his eyes gleamed demonically. "Prove it."

Unable to drum up an answering smile she huddled down in the seat, listless with defeat. The day, which had started out so full of anticipation, had sunk too far in disappointment to be redeemed with humor and she was beyond fighting to save it. She just wanted it to be over.

As he swung the car around, the headlights sliced across the landscape, turning the rain to long silver darning needles spearing the night. "We passed a motel about ten miles back. Let's hope the road hasn't washed out between here and there, and that they still have vacancies."

Luck was with them, but barely. The motel had been built in the fifties and hadn't seen a dollar spent on it since. A bare bulb hung above the desk in the office. Tears in the vinyl padding on the one chair were held together with duct tape. The manager, Lily noticed with a shudder, reeked of tobacco and had tufts of hair growing out of his ears, which left him looking like a troll.

"Busy night tonight, what with the weather and all," he told them. "Only got the one room left. Take it or leave it, folks. You don't want it, someone else will."

"We'll take it," Sebastian said, slapping down a credit card and filling out the registration card.

"I'm not spending the night in the same room with

you,'' Lily informed him, trailing behind as he marched to their assigned unit.

''You'd rather sleep in the car?''

''*No!*''

He unlocked door number nineteen and flung it open. ''Well, I'm not offering to, if that's what you're hoping, so step inside and make yourself at home while I unload our stuff.''

''Sebastian,'' she exclaimed, still hovering on the threshold when he returned with her luggage, a zippered nylon sports bag, and a newspaper, ''this place is a flea pit!''

He reined in a sigh. ''So sorry it isn't up to the five-star standards you were probably hoping for, but it's warm and dry, isn't it? There's a shower and a bed.''

Exactly. *One* bed! Not a bed and a pull-out sofa, not even an armchair. Just a double mattress that sagged in the middle and was covered by an ugly green bedspread, which had seen better days. The only other furniture consisted of a nightstand holding a fake wood reading lamp, a ratty chest of drawers with a TV on top, and a straight-back chair that matched the one in the office, even down to the duct tape patching.

''I'm not sleeping on that bed!''

He shrugged. ''Sack out on the floor then.''

Not an inviting prospect, either. There were suspicious stains on the threadbare carpet. ''You're the most insensitive creature I've ever met!''

''And you're a spoiled brat.'' Kicking the door closed, he dumped her suitcases next to it, tossed the sports bag and newspaper on the bed, and shrugged out of his jacket. His shoes and socks came off next, followed by his tie.

She watched in sly fascination as he proceeded to peel off his shirt, thereby displaying an expanse of muscular,

well-tanned chest and proof positive that his width of
shoulder owed nothing to clever tailoring. Well, if he
thought flexing his pecs would impress her, he was in for
a disappointment! It would take more than that to get a
rise out of her.

Just how little more she soon found out. "What do you
think you're doing?" she squeaked in horror, when he
casually began unbuckling the belt holding up his pants.

"I'd have thought it was obvious. I'm getting out of
these wet clothes, and then I'm taking a shower. Close
your mouth and stop gaping, Ms. Talbot."

"I don't believe…what I'm seeing!"

"Then don't look."

The belt was off, the zipper of his fly sliding down.
The next second, he was shucking his trousers as unself-
consciously as if he were completely alone. And for the
life of her, she couldn't look away.

He glanced up and caught her staring. "You're blush-
ing, Ms. Talbot."

Any fool could see that! "Well, one of us certainly
should be, and it clearly isn't going to be you."

He had great legs. Wonderful thighs. Lean, muscular,
tanned. Long, strong, powerful. And he preferred briefs
to boxers. Plain white cotton to silk stripes and fancy colors.

"Don't you *dare* remove anything else!" she said
hoarsely. "I'm not interested in seeing you in the altogether."

"Just as well," he said, folding his trousers over the
back of the chair. "I don't show my altogether to just
anyone."

He draped his jacket over a wire hanger in the curtained
recess that passed for a closet then did the same for his
shirt. And she, ninny that she was, followed his every

move and wondered how it was that God had seen fit to bless men with such trim, taut hips, even if the rest of them was oversized!

"Sure you don't want to use the bathroom?"

"Quite sure, thank you. There's probably an inch of mold growing in the tub."

"No tub," he said, almost gleefully, poking his head around the door to inspect. "Just a shower stall."

"I wish you the joy of it."

"I'm sure you do." He flung a glance over his shoulder and she could have sworn he was biting back a snicker. "No peeking, Ms. Talbot, and no funny business."

"Funny business?"

"There isn't room for two in here. If you change your mind about taking a shower, wait your turn."

"Oh, dream on!" she gasped, flabbergasted by his gall. "Heaven only knows what might come crawling up the drain."

But the truth was, her clothes were sticking to her most uncomfortably, her skin felt unpleasantly clammy and the idea of standing under a hot shower didn't seem such a bad idea, after all. She had fresh underwear and a nightshirt in her suitcase; dry clothes she could pull out for tomorrow. Who was she really punishing by stubbornly refusing to make the best of the situation?

Sebastian reappeared ten minutes later, wearing a skimpy towel draped perilously around his hips and nothing else. His black hair stood up in spikes, drops of water gleamed on his skin, and he smelled of clean, warm man. "The place might be a flea pit, but at least there's plenty of hot water. Sure you don't want to take advantage of it?"

She cleared her throat. "I might." She eyed his makeshift loincloth, then hastily glanced away again.

"There's another towel in there, if that's what you're wondering," he said snidely.

"Good," she croaked and fled with the toiletry bag, nightshirt and panties she'd taken from her suitcase.

In keeping with the rest of the place, the bathroom was basic: a washbasin, a toilet and a fiberglass shower stall with a mottled glass door. An unused towel the same size as the one barely covering the delectable Sebastian Caine lay folded on a shelf, and the management had kindly provided a minuscule bar of soap, a tiny bottle of shampoo, most of which he'd used, and two paper cups.

Fortunately she came fully equipped with hand-milled French soap, body lotion, salon formula shampoo and conditioner and, praise heaven, toothbrush and paste. She wasted no time putting them all to good use.

From the feel of them, the pillows were stuffed with peanut shells, and the mattress wasn't a whole lot better. But it beat a marble slab in the nearest morgue, which was where they'd almost certainly have wound up if he hadn't spotted the washed-out bridge when he did.

He'd been rattled, and he didn't mind admitting it. But her reaction had been over the top! Jumping out of the car like that and racing off without the first idea where she was headed pretty much proved his first impression had been right: the woman spelled nothing but trouble. Still, he hadn't been able to help feeling sorry for her. She'd been trembling like a leaf when he finally caught up with her, and the way she'd felt when he'd picked her up...

Best not to dwell too long on how she felt—or looked. His mandate was to deliver the goods, not sample them! Which reminded him Hugo would be expecting them to show up at the house anytime now.

Jamming a pillow behind his head, he stretched out on the mattress, pulled the top sheet up to his waist and reached for the phone.

Hugo picked up on the first ring. "Sebastian?"

"How'd you guess?"

"I saw the weather report on television. The whole county's under siege with this rain. You'll never make it up here tonight."

"I'm way ahead of you, Hugo. We checked into a motel about an hour ago."

"Thank God! So both you and Lily are safe?"

No point in regaling him with their close call. No point, either, in entering into a debate about the dubious wisdom of daughter and stepson spending the night together. "We're safe."

"So tell me, how do you like her, now that you know her a bit better?"

"She's…" *Nosy. Annoying. Too smart-mouthed for her own good.* And, he was beginning to realize, *sexy as all get-out!* "Hell, you know me, Hugo. I don't jump to conclusions until I've got all the facts."

Hugo laughed. "Just once in your life, could you try not to behave so much like a lawyer?"

And do what? Take advantage of the situation and put the moves on her? Better stick to being a lawyer! "It's who I am, you know that."

"I want the two of you to get along. We're all family here, Sebastian."

"Which is precisely why I'm being cautious. You've always been like a father to me, Hugo. Now it's my turn to act like a son and protect your interests."

"You're worrying about nothing. Lily doesn't have any ulterior motives for seeking me out."

"Uh-huh." No point in stating the obvious: that she

was her mother's daughter. Even if genetics weren't a factor, her role model had been a woman without conscience or moral rectitude. All that being so, who could say what motivated her actions? Only time would reveal that.

"Is she as pretty as she looks in the photo she sent?"

Just then, the bathroom door opened and Lily emerged on a cloud of steamy, flower-scented air. Her skin was flushed—and he ought to know. Enough of it was showing.

"Sebastian?" Hugo's voice came from a great distance. "Are you still there?"

"Yeah." He cleared his throat and dragged his gaze away from the hem of the pale blue nightshirt, which barely covered her backside. How come she didn't smell of cheap motel soap, the way he did? How come she looked as if she'd been polished with moon dust? Why was her damp hair so lush and lustrous-looking that he wanted to take handfuls of it and let it slide through his fingers?

"Well? Is she?"

Dry-mouthed, he said, "Is who what?"

"Is Lily as pretty as her picture?"

She came to the foot of the bed and stood with her hands behind her back, looking for all the world about fifteen years old. Well below the age of consent! "Shall I wait in the bathroom until you've finished your call?" she whispered.

"No," he said, answering them both at once. The photo Hugo was referring to had been a snapshot taken at a distance and had revealed only sketchy details. Addressing his stepfather again, he added, "I'd say 'different.'"

"Better?"

"Different," he said firmly. "Look, Hugo, I'll call you in the morning, once I've checked the road report. Sleep well and don't worry about us. One way or another, we'll make it home tomorrow."

"Why didn't you say it was Hugo on the line?" she started in, the minute he hung up. "I'd have liked to speak to him."

"He knew I was calling from a motel room."

"So?"

"I didn't think you'd want him to know you were sharing it with me."

"Why not if, as you claim, it's an unavoidable and perfectly innocent arrangement?"

"Because I'm not so sure it is innocent. If it were, you wouldn't be parading around half-naked."

Her pupils flared and she heaved a breath that set her breasts to bouncing gently beneath her nightshirt. "You've got some nerve! What about you flaunting nothing but a towel?"

He jerked aside the sheet and rather enjoyed the way she reared back in alarm. "You'll notice I've exchanged it for a perfectly decent pair of swimming trunks."

Which fit snugly enough to discourage untoward activity in his nether regions!

"I wondered what you had hidden in that sports bag," she said, recovering quickly.

"Now you know."

"And are swimming trunks all you're planning to wear to bed?"

"Afraid so. I forgot to bring a top hat."

"Very funny, I'm sure!"

He shrugged. "I aim to please."

She gave a huffing little sniff, which told him exactly

what she thought of his pathetic sense of humor. "Move over to your own side. You're on my half of the bed."

"I thought you said you wouldn't sully your body by laying it on this mattress?"

"Upon consideration, I've decided the bed's safer than the floor."

She wouldn't want to bet money on it, if she knew the direction his thoughts kept taking!

She turned back the top sheet, using only the tips of her fingers as if she expected something to leap out and bite her. "This isn't exactly the kind of place I expected to be spending the night."

"Relax," he said. "I already chased away the bed bugs."

Her eyes, large and luminous to begin with, widened to saucer size. "Is that another of your feeble jokes?"

"Hell, no! They were marching heel to toe over the pillow, big as fighter jets, some of them—but they didn't hold a candle to the cockroaches tap dancing on the floor."

She yelped and leaped onto the mattress. It creaked ominously, formed an even more pronounced sag in the middle and sent her rolling toward him. One minute, he was lying there keeping his distance, and the next, she was pressed up against him with nothing but her abbreviated nightshirt coming between them.

She smelled even better, up close. As for the way she felt...! Silky, smooth as cream, soft. The way nature intended a woman to feel, with just enough meat on her bones to turn her angles into sweet, alluring curves.

Intending to shove her back where she belonged, he closed his hands over her shoulders and managed to choke out, "You're trespassing."

But that's as far as he got because he made the mistake

of looking at her face. Her features were delicate as porcelain, her brows finely shaped, her lashes so long and thick they looked artificial. And her eyes...

He fought to breathe normally and tried to look away. A man could lose his soul staring into those eyes.

"If you don't like it—" she began, sounding as if she, too, had just run a marathon.

"I don't!"

"Then let me go."

Easier said than done! He didn't trust her and he didn't like her, but underneath his lawyerly facade he was still only a man and there were some things beyond his control. Such as his hands, one of which slid from her shoulder to her jaw and from there to her hair, while the other stroked over her bare arm. And his mouth, which suddenly itched to taste hers. And not to be outperformed, an uprising from that singular component of the male anatomy which most definitely sported a mind of its own.

Show a little decency and move away, for crying out loud! his mind commanded.

But beneath the drooping veil of her lashes, her eyes had turned dreamy. Her lips had fallen softly apart. The hard points of her nipples pressed against his chest. Her thighs nested warmly against his.

We're all family, Sebastian...I want you to get along....

But not quite this well!

She was the one to break the spell, if that's what it could be called. "I told you this wasn't a good idea," she said faintly.

"So you did."

"Perhaps now, you'll believe me."

Masking his reluctance, he let go of her and rolled onto his back. "I never disputed the fact. But neither did I expect you'd fling yourself at me the way you just did."

"That was a regrettable accident."

"The way I see it," he said, glaring at her, "the entire business of your being here at all is regrettable."

He thought himself well-armed against her, that nothing she might say or do would breach his defenses, but the sudden hurt in her eyes stirred him to dangerous compassion. Damn her for invading his part of the world! Why couldn't she have stayed where she belonged?

Gritting his teeth, he snapped off the lamp, folded his hands behind his head and stared at the ceiling. He'd hoped for utter darkness, something to erase his awareness of the shape of her lying beside him, but a floodlight on top of a pole in the parking area shone directly at the window, spearing the thin fabric of the curtains and filling the room with a dim glow.

A silence descended, oppressive with unspoken tension. Time trickled past—fifteen minutes, half an hour.

She lay ramrod straight, arms by her sides, legs held primly together. Only her breasts moved, rising faintly with her every breath, but she wasn't sleeping. Slewing his gaze, he caught the gleam of her open eyes in the murky light, and then, to his horror, saw a tear slip down her cheek.

He pretended not to notice. No more anxious to acknowledge her distress than he was, she turned her face away and he thought the danger had passed. But then a faint sniff pierced the silence, followed by a smothered gulp.

Finally he could stand it no longer. "Why are you crying?"

"Because," she said, after a wrenching pause, "I miss my mother and dad. Just when I think I've come to terms with losing them, it hits me all over again. I guess I must be overtired or something, because I seem to be doing a lot of crying lately.''

Was it her referring to her mother's second husband as ''dad'' that softened him, or was he just a pushover when it came to women in distress? Whatever the reason, he found himself wanting to comfort her. ''I'm sorry if I came across as an unfeeling lout earlier. I know how hard it is to lose a parent,'' he admitted. ''My father died when I was eight.''

Slowly she wriggled onto her back again. ''It hurts, doesn't it, no matter how old a person is?''

''Yes,'' he said, not sure he liked the near-intimacy of skin touching skin the sagging mattress enforced, but not exactly objecting to it, either. ''At first, I refused to believe I'd never see him again. I used to look for him in crowds. Every time there was a knock at the door or the phone rang, I'd expect it to be him. I remember the first Christmas without him, the first birthday, the first vacation, and how much I envied those kids who had both parents around to take them places and do things with.''

''Were you an only child?''

''Yes,'' he said, and went on to tell her how he'd gradually come to terms with his loss.

After a while, though, it occurred to him that he was the one doing all the talking when he should be taking advantage of such a heaven-sent opportunity to learn more about her. ''I gather you were a pretty close-knit family,'' he said. ''Were you still living at home when you lost your parents?''

He waited for her to reply and when she didn't, he raised his head a fraction to look at her and saw that she'd fallen asleep with her cheek lightly brushing his shoulder. She looked young and innocent and totally at peace.

He wished he could drift off as easily, but his thoughts

were too chaotic. Facts on which he'd based all his assumptions about her suddenly appeared less well-founded and he hated the uncertainty it produced.

Part of him wanted her to be exactly as she appeared: a young woman with nothing in mind but coping with personal tragedy and getting to know the man who'd fathered her. But another, greater part clung to the legal training in which it was so well versed and warned him not to be lulled into a false sense of security.

So she'd shed a tear or two and shown a more vulnerable side. What did that prove except that there was more to her than initially met the eye? Underneath, she was still the same unknown quantity; a woman with a questionable agenda.

I'd love to come and stay with you, she'd told Hugo, latching on to his invitation with unsettling alacrity. *There's nothing to keep me in Vancouver right now, nothing at all. Discovering you couldn't have come at a better time.*

Better for whom, and why? Not for Hugo, who'd been put through enough by her money-grubbing mother, and who'd fought hard for the good life he now enjoyed. No prodigal daughter showing up on the doorstep was going to spoil that, not as long as Sebastian Caine was around to monitor events!

She sighed in her sleep and kicked at the sheet so that it slipped down to expose the top of her thighs and the pale line of the panties she was wearing under her nightshirt.

Carefully he lifted his wrist and pressed the button to illuminate the face of his watch. Not yet eleven o'clock. Another six hours before daylight and the chance to assess the storm's damage. Another six hours of lying next to her and feeling her perfumed warmth reach out to touch him.

There was a hell, and the devil ruled!

CHAPTER THREE

THEY reached Stentonbridge shortly before lunch the next day. A small town nestled on the banks of a wide river, it boasted quiet residential streets shaded by old maples and lined with elegant nineteenth-century houses. But nothing quite prepared Lily for the opulence of the Preston estate.

Situated on several acres of riverfront property, the house sat in majestic Georgian splendor on a low rise, amid manicured lawns and lush flower beds. "Why, it's beautiful!" she exclaimed, taking in the spectacle as the car swept up to the front entrance.

"As you very well knew it would be," Sebastian said dryly. "You received photos, I'm sure."

"But they didn't do the place justice. Nothing could. It's...palatial! It must cost Hugo a fortune to maintain these gardens." She shook her head ruefully. "I wish I was the one supplying his stock."

"Try to control the dollar signs dancing in your eyes, Ms. Talbot, and remember why you're supposed to be here. The welcoming committee will descend any minute now, and I'll be seriously ticked off if the first words out of your mouth imply the only thing you're interested in is how much Hugo's worth."

She'd woken that morning feeling well rested and optimistic, with the emotional overload of the past night behind her. Foolishly she'd hoped she and Sebastian had reached some sort of truce and his sly insinuations were at an end. But for all that the new day had brought clear skies, from the moment he'd opened his eyes his disposition had been anything but sunny. Perhaps, she'd thought at the time, he just wasn't a morning person and his mood would eventually improve.

If anything, though, it worsened. When she'd thanked him for his sympathetic understanding of the night before, he'd shrugged her off with a succinctness that bordered on surly. He'd reacted with near contempt to her enthusiasm for the charming old towns they passed through. Refusing to let him dampen her spirits, she'd remained doggedly cheerful. This latest attack, though, was not something she felt inclined to let pass.

"I resent that remark, Sebastian. It's completely uncalled for."

"Is it? When I woke up this morning, you were pawing through the money I'd left lying on the dresser in that motel room."

"I was not! I was looking for your keys so that I could load my luggage in the trunk of your car and be ready to leave the second you decreed we should, as you very well know because I explained it the minute you started leveling accusations at me. And if you'd got up at a reasonable hour, instead of lying around in bed half the morning, I wouldn't have had occasion to *paw* through anything belonging to you!"

"I hardly call getting up at eight o'clock and being on the road by nine 'lying around in bed half the morning.'"

"I was up at six."

"I didn't get to sleep until nearly four."

"Well, don't take your insomnia out on me!" she snapped, so exasperated she was ready to crown him with her purse. "It's not my fault."

"Lower your voice and stop waving your arms around

like that," he said. "In case you haven't noticed, we have an audience."

She saw then that the front door of the house stood open and, suddenly, all the silly bickering didn't matter anymore. "Is that Hugo?" she whispered, her gaze glued to the white-haired man coming down the steps with a silky English setter dancing at his heels.

"Afraid so," Sebastian said. "Disappointed it's not the butler?"

"No," she cooed sweetly. "But I wish the dog was a rottweiler and you were its lunch."

"Nice," he said. "Very nice, Ms. Talbot. You're finally showing your true colors."

Smiling determinedly, she hissed, "Why don't you go jump in the river, Sebastian?" and without waiting for him to hurl something equally rude back at her, climbed out of the car and walked toward the man waiting at the foot of the steps.

Hugo Preston was almost seventy but didn't look a day over sixty. Tall and erect, with an enviable head of silver hair and clear blue eyes, he cut a handsome figure. "Well, Lily," he said warmly as she approached, "we meet at last!"

"Yes," she said, all at once awash with conflicting emotions. How did a woman greet the man whose blood ran in her veins but who, for reasons he'd yet to disclose, had chosen to remain incognito until recently? With a kiss, a handshake, a hug?

What did she call him, now that they were meeting face-to-face? Given his dignified bearing, *Hugo* suddenly seemed too familiar, and *Mr. Preston* absurdly formal...but *Dad?* Neil Talbot had been the man who'd filled that role, and her ties to him were too strong to be so easily severed in favor of this smiling stranger.

Seeming to sense her uncertainty, Hugo took her hands and kissed her lightly on both cheeks. "My dear daughter, you have no idea what today means to me. I would be deeply honored if, in time, you could bring yourself to call me Father. Until then, I'm Hugo...and this," he continued, turning to the slender blond woman who'd come out to join him, "is Cynthia, my wife."

Cynthia Preston did not fit the image of The Other Woman. Even less did she look or act the part of resentful stepmother. Tall and elegant in a pale bronze two-piece ensemble with gold accessories, she was, quite simply, beautiful. More than that, she was kind. It showed in her smile, and in her sky-blue eyes.

"I'm so happy to meet you, Lily," she said, enveloping her in a warm hug. "Hugo has hoped for a long time that this day would come. We both have. And we're so grateful to you for making it possible. Welcome to our home and please forgive our dog for pawing you like that. She considers herself one of the family."

Such total acceptance, following on the heels of Sebastian's trenchant disapproval, completely undid Lily and, to her embarrassment, she burst into tears. "Thank you," she wailed, dripping all over Cynthia's fine silk shirt. "I'm really...very h-happy to be here."

"No more than we are to have you." Slipping an arm around her waist, Cynthia guided her up the steps. "What a dreadful time you had of it yesterday. We were so worried when we heard the news. Let's go inside and I'll show you where you can freshen up, then we'll have lunch and start to get properly acquainted. Sebastian, bring in Lily's luggage, will you, and take it up to the Rose Room?"

If she hadn't found herself such an emotional mess, Lily would have enjoyed watching the almighty Sebastian

Caine reduced to the role of porter. But she was too busy mopping up her tears on the linen handkerchief Hugo had produced and trying not to smudge her mascara in the process. She'd taken great pains with her appearance that morning just so that she'd make a good first impression, and here she was, all red-nosed and puffy-eyed within minutes of arriving!

"I'm not normally like this," she said apologetically.

"Nor are we," Cynthia replied. "But look, Hugo and I are both misty-eyed, too. Family reunions tend to have this effect on people."

Unless your name happened to be Sebastian Caine! Lily felt his glare on the back of her neck as he tramped up the stairs with her suitcases, and wondered how he'd manage to sit through the meal and not let fly with one of his barbed remarks.

As it happened, she worried needlessly. He had someone else to occupy his attention. When Lily joined the rest of the family on the terrace after splashing cold water on her face and running a comb through her hair in the guest powder room, she found another woman had joined the party, and that she considered Sebastian her personal property became immediately apparent.

"Hello, I'm Penny Stanford," she said, subjecting Lily to a somewhat clinical inspection. "I wanted to be on hand to meet the long-lost daughter who stole my man away last night."

Oh, please, you're welcome to every miserable inch of him! Lily wanted to say. *Oh, and by the way, did you know he has another girlfriend stashed away in the city, and she looks ready to give birth any day now?*

Instead she confined her reply to a noncommittal "How nice to meet you."

"I think we could all use a little sherry before we sit

down to eat,'' Hugo decided. "You and Penny will join us, won't you, Sebastian?"

"No, thanks," he said. "I've got a load of paperwork to take care of at the office and Penny's working the night shift tonight so she needs to get some sleep."

"I'm head nurse on the surgical floor at our local hospital," she informed Lily grandly.

"I sell flowers," Lily said.

"How nice." Nurse Penny swatted at the English setter. "Do stop sniffing at me like that, Katie! It's so unhygienic. Well, Sebastian, since I left my car at the stables, I'll hop a ride over there with you. Shall we go?"

"Sure." His glance skimmed over Lily. "Enjoy lunch."

Cynthia looked up from her chaise. "You'll be here for dinner, won't you, Sebastian?"

"I hadn't planned on it."

"But it's Lily's first evening here and I'd like the whole family on hand to make it special." She paused and sent him a sly little smile. "I had fresh lobster brought in, and Clara's making your favorite dessert."

"That's shameless bribery," Hugo chuckled, pouring the sherry. "The man has his own life, Cynthia, and there'll be other nights."

"And he's already done more than his share to make me feel welcome," Lily put in blandly. "Please, Sebastian, don't feel you have to show up on my account. I'll be perfectly happy without you, so consider yourself excused."

"Lobster, you say?" Glacial as a northern sky in winter, his gaze once again settled on Lily.

Cynthia nodded. "And raspberry tart. With homemade vanilla ice cream. A meal fit for a king, Sebastian—or, in this case, our new princess."

"Count me in, then. I wouldn't miss it for the world."

The satisfaction in his voice left Lily in no doubt about who'd emerged the winner in this latest go-round. She should have kept her mouth shut, instead of baiting him like that!

"I've got to get to the office and return some calls." He dropped a kiss on his mother's cheek. "What time are you serving dinner?"

"Half past seven, the same as usual. But come early if you can."

"Will Natalie be here?"

"Of course. She can't wait to meet Lily." Cynthia waved Sebastian and Penny off, then turned to Lily. "Natalie's taking extra summer courses at our local college and had a class she couldn't afford to miss this morning. She asked me to pass on her apologies for not being here to greet you, but she'll be home by three o'clock, which gives you time for a bit of a rest after lunch before you meet her."

"I look forward to it," Lily said. "What's she studying?"

"She wants to be a social worker. It's been her dream since she was a little girl. She'd like to work with children. But she can tell you all about that herself. Your father and I are more interested in learning about you. You're a horticulturist, right?"

Lily grimaced self-deprecatingly. "I'm just a florist. Until recently, I was part-owner of a retail outlet."

"So you know your flowers, which makes you very much your father's daughter! I've always said, if Hugo hadn't been in the legal profession, he'd have been a professional gardener."

Rising gracefully from her chaise, Cynthia ushered Lily to the umbrella-shaded table and waited for Hugo to seat them both before picking up the conversation again. "I gather from your remark, Lily, that you're no longer in business for yourself?"

"My colleague and I dissolved our partnership," she said, choosing her words carefully. Despite the warm welcome she'd received, she was among strangers. How would they receive the news that Jonathan Speirs, the mousy little accountant who was her business associate and who took care of all the bookkeeping, had been arrested for fraud, money laundering and connections to organized crime, and that, because of their business connection, she herself had been thrown under suspicion of conspiracy?

Sebastian, she knew, would have a field day, and with some cause!

The trouble with cases like this, her lawyer had told her, when the magnitude of Jonathan's criminal activities had first come to light, *is that people tend to forget which one's the guilty party and you both wind up being splattered with dirt. The police are pretty much convinced you're not involved in Speirs's activities, but you are a material witness, and I'd prefer you put as much distance between yourself and him as possible. It's a good time for you to get out of town until the case goes to trial, which won't be until after the summer.*

Cynthia dipped the bowl of her sterling spoon into her chilled watercress soup. "Does that mean you're working for someone else now, Lily?"

"No. I leased temporary premises from a friend so that I could honor promises I'd already made to do the flowers for several May and June weddings, but now that they're over, my time's my own."

"So there's no urgent reason for you to rush back to Vancouver?"

"Cynthia," Hugo interrupted, pouring white wine into fine crystal stemware, "I thought we agreed not to pressure Lily into making any long-term decisions until she's had a chance to get used to us."

"Letting her know there's no time limit on her stay isn't pressure, Hugo darling," she said lightly. "It's telling her she's family and this is her home. What's so bad about that? Heaven knows, this house is big enough to accommodate one more!"

"Does Sebastian live here?" Lily asked, jumping at the chance to ask a question she'd had in mind ever since she met him.

"Not quite," Hugo told her. "He lives in the old groom's quarters above the stables, which lie quite a distance from the main house. We often don't see him from one week to the next. The only one left at home is Natalie."

Well that, at least, was a bonus! The idea of tripping over Sebastian every time she set foot out of her room held no appeal at all.

Noticing that she'd finished her soup, Cynthia passed her a platter of fat prawns. "Try some of these, Lily."

"They look delicious, but I'll pass, thanks."

"You're not hungry?"

"I thought I was," she confessed, stifling an unladylike yawn, "but the sun and the wine are making me sleepy."

"Then you must rest. Don't blame the weather or the wine, dear. It's all that traveling, and the dreadful time you had yesterday." She put aside her napkin and stood up. "Come with me and I'll show you to your room."

She led Lily through the house and up the grand staircase. "Just let me know if there's anything you need," she said, standing back to allow her entrance to a large corner suite at the end of the upper hall.

"I can't imagine there will be," Lily said, taking in the luxury awaiting her. "This room is absolutely lovely, Cynthia."

Cynthia permitted herself a small smile. "I like to keep things looking nice. If you need anything ironed before you dress for dinner, just let me know."

So the family dressed for dinner! Grateful for the subtle hint and glad she'd brought along a couple of dressy outfits, Lily thanked her, closed the door and set about exploring her new surroundings.

The suite was charming, with four tall windows draped in deep rose taffeta on two of the walls. One side offered a view of the gardens and the river. The other overlooked a swimming pool and, showing through the trees some distance away, the gabled roof of another, smaller building.

The walls were covered in pale pink silk, there were roses in a silver bowl on a small pedestal table next to an armchair upholstered in pale pink velvet, and on the Queen Anne desk in the corner. The off-white carpet was deep and luxurious, the bed an antique four-poster flanked by bow-fronted nightstands of similar vintage, the paintings on the walls exquisite flower prints mounted in gold leaf frames.

Double doors led to a large, equally opulent bathroom. "Good grief!" Lily exclaimed, standing on the threshold. "A person could hold a party in here and still have room to spare!"

She eyed the deep marble tub longingly, but decided to postpone the pleasure of bathing until after she'd taken a nap. Sebastian Caine was coming for dinner, and she wanted to be well rested before they squared off again. Shedding her sandals and dress, she climbed onto the bed, nestled against the soft feather pillows and took stock of the morning's events.

Sebastian found his mother and sister on the terrace when he got to the main house that evening, but there was no sign of Hugo or Lily Talbot.

"Daddy took her off to the library," Natalie informed him. "They're probably talking about the past."

"But you've met her?"

"Yes."

"And?"

"I love her! She's exactly the way I hoped she'd be— so pretty and nice and friendly. I really feel as if we're sisters."

Raising his brows, he glanced at his mother.

"Don't look at me like that," she said. "I happen to agree with Natalie. I know you've got your doubts, Sebastian, but Lily really does seem genuine. Although..."

"Although what?" Suspicions on full alert, he regarded her closely.

"She did mention, in a roundabout sort of way at lunch, that she's out of work. But that isn't necessarily significant."

"You think not, do you?"

"Honestly, Sebastian!" Natalie scoffed. "You're always looking for the worst in people!"

"And you're always looking for the best—even when it's obvious to everyone else that it isn't to be found."

She set her mouth in the stubborn cast he knew so well. "Oh, phooey! Why can't you be like the rest of us and just take Lily at face value?"

"Because somebody around here has to dig beneath the surface."

"Why? What's she ever done to you that you're so set against her?"

"It's what she might do to you that worries me, Nat."

She threw up her hands in disgust. "Such as what? Steal my jewelry when I'm not looking? Poison my food? This isn't a fairy tale, and I'm not Cinderella at the mercy of a wicked stepsister. Your trouble is, you spend too much time around criminals, Sebastian. You need to get a life."

"I'm a divorce lawyer," he said, grinning at her outburst. Natalie had always been a spitfire when it came to defending anyone she perceived to be the underdog. "I don't come across too many felons in my particular line of work, though there has been the odd one, I must admit. But I pride myself on being a pretty good judge of character."

She snorted disparagingly. "If you were, you wouldn't be squiring Penny Stanford around town!"

"Penny's harmless."

"That just goes to show how much you know! She's so busy sinking her hooks into you, I'm surprised you don't need a weekly blood transfusion!"

Penny might be trying to land him, but she wasn't even close to succeeding. More to the point, she was no threat to his peace of mind, whereas Lily Talbot...!

The object of his displeasure chose that moment to swan out to the terrace on Hugo's arm. Although he didn't profess to be an expert in haute couture, Sebastian knew quality when he saw it, and the flame-red chiffon gown clinging lovingly to Lily's curves wasn't something she'd picked up in the bargain basement of the nearest department store. The whole outfit, down to the matching silk pumps, and pearl-and-garnet choker and earrings, was a custom affair designed to make the most of her looks.

She was laughing at something Hugo had said, and he was clearly besotted with her. The animation faded from her face when she saw Sebastian, though. "Oh, you're here," she said, plainly wishing he were anywhere but. "I half expected you'd change your mind about joining us."

"Wishful thinking on your part, I'm afraid, Ms. Talbot," he informed her, wondering how she managed such an extravagant wardrobe on a florist's earnings. Either she'd inherited a bundle when her parents died, or she had some other source of income, and it was the *some other* that piqued his curiosity!

"Ms. Talbot?" Nat hooted, oblivious to the undercurrents swirling in the atmosphere. "What a lot of pompous nonsense! For heaven's sake, Sebastian, why don't you call her 'Lily' like the rest of us?"

"Yes," Lily said, playing the innocent for all she was worth. "Why don't you, Sebastian? After all, we're family."

He'd have wrung her pretty neck if it weren't that the rest of them would have rushed to her defense. *Because we're not family and I don't intend to roll over and play dead on your say-so,* he thought. "Neither of you has a drink," he said, smoothly changing the subject. "What'll you have, Hugo? Your usual?"

"Not tonight. In honor of the occasion, I'll join Cynthia and Natalie and have champagne." He turned to Lily. "What about you, my dear?"

"I never turn down champagne," she said, practically simpering at him.

Grinding his teeth, Sebastian grabbed the neck of the bottle of Montrachet, hoisted it from the ice bucket and filled two flutes. Under cover of handing one to Lily, he cupped her elbow in his hand and steered her out of hearing range of the others. "What were you and Hugo talking about in the library while my mother and sister were left out here cooling their heels?"

"*My* mother. The *first* Mrs. Preston," she said defiantly, shrugging him off. "In other words, none of your business, Sebastian."

"As long as you're a guest under the roof of the present and *last* Mrs. Preston, I'm making it my business. And I won't tolerate your challenging my mother's right to be in this house."

"If your mother were one-tenth as boorish as you, I'd be staying in a hotel. As it is, I find her an utterly charming hostess and I wouldn't dream of insulting her. Or of hurting her feelings by telling her what I think of her son!"

He'd made her angry. Her cheeks were delicately flushed. Her parted lips were the same color as the flamered begonias growing on the shaded north side of the stables. Without warning, he found himself wondering if they'd feel as silky smooth as they looked, and what she'd do if he suddenly bent down and kissed her.

Before he could act on such an insane notion, Cynthia joined them. "What are you two whispering about?"

"I was admiring your lovely home," Lily said. "You have exquisite taste. Have you always lived here?"

"Only since I married Hugo. Before that, Sebastian and I lived in Hamilton, in an apartment. Rather a nice one, to be sure, but it didn't compare to this."

"Not many places would, I suspect." Lily smiled, and Sebastian could practically hear the calculator clicking into gear behind those big, guileless brown eyes.

"I'll take you on a tour after dinner, if you like," his mother offered, completely drawn in. "Hugo grew up here, but he gave me a free hand redecorating the place when we married and I'm rather proud of the job I did.''

"So it's been in the Preston family a long time?''

"Yes,'' his mother replied, blithely ignoring the warning glance Sebastian shot her way. "His great-great-grandfather had the house built in the late 1840s and every generation of Prestons since was born here.''

Lily sipped her champagne reflectively, then said, "It's odd to think they were all my ancestors and I didn't even know they existed until recently.''

"I know your father would love to tell you what he knows of them, but it'll have to wait until another time. Sebastian, will you take Lily in to dinner? I believe we're ready to be served.''

Given little other choice, he tucked her hand under his elbow and led her into the house. Her perfume teased him faintly, an alluring, exotic scent reminiscent of tropical flowers; plumeria or tuberose, he thought. Even though she was wearing heels, his height advantage allowed him a covert glimpse of her cleavage.

A flash of heat caught him off guard, riding over him to settle low in his belly. Furious, he transferred his gaze elsewhere and wished he could as easily divert other, less biddable sections of his anatomy. But the unpalatable truth was, although he mistrusted her, he mistrusted himself more. The more he saw of her, the more desirable he found her.

Well, there was one sure way to put an end to that nonsense. First thing tomorrow, he'd make some calls to the West Coast and initiate an investigation into her background. Hugo wouldn't like it; had openly forbidden any such move, in fact. But in this case, what Hugo might learn could well end up hurting him a lot less than what he didn't know.

"I've put Lily on her father's right, and Natalie on his left next to you," his mother said, taking her customary place.

At least, he'd be spared having to sit next to the woman throughout the meal, he thought, depositing her with relief at her chair and taking his place on the other side of the long table. But sitting opposite her brought its own share of hazards. Try though he might to find diversion elsewhere, he couldn't help watching her.

She had a habit of pressing her lips together after she'd taken a sip of wine. He found himself waiting for that mannerism with absurd anticipation. He had seldom seen a more delectable mouth. It could ruin a man, if he let it.

"Don't you agree, Sebastian?"

"Huh?" Jerking his attention back to safer channels, he realized he hadn't the first idea what had prompted his mother's question.

"Hel...*lo!*" Natalie chanted. "We're talking about Daddy's birthday, big brother, and you get to cast the deciding vote. What's it to be?"

"I'll go along with whatever Hugo wants."

"Then it's settled." Cynthia looked pleased. "We'll throw a joint party here a week from Saturday, to celebrate Hugo's turning seventy and to welcome Lily to Stentonbridge, then go up to the cottage later in the month. I'll get on to the caterer tomorrow."

"I'd love to take care of the flowers," Lily said. "If you don't mind letting me loose in the garden, that is."

"Not in the least," Hugo assured her. "You're welcome to whatever you fancy, my dear, including the greenhouse stock."

"And we need to think of someone to be Lily's escort," Cynthia said. "I'd ask you, Sebastian, but I don't think Penny would be too happy about lending you out for the evening.''

Ignoring Nat's unladylike titter, he said, ''Probably not.''

''Never mind. I'm sure there are plenty of eligible bachelors in town who'd be only too delighted to take on the job.''

He had no doubt about it, either. And the idea was enough to put him off his food, steamed lobster and raspberry tart notwithstanding.

CHAPTER FOUR

IT DIDN'T sit too well with Lily, either. "Heavens, this is the twenty-first century! I don't need a blind date to see me through the evening. I'm quite well able to look after myself." She dabbed her perfect mouth with her napkin and purposefully changed the subject. "You mentioned a cottage, Cynthia?"

"Yes. We have a summer place on the lake, about an hour's drive from here. Unfortunately we don't use it nearly as much as we did when the children were young, but it's a lovely peaceful spot and I think you'll enjoy seeing it."

"I don't know why you don't sell the place," Sebastian said. "The upkeep's more trouble than it's worth."

"I guess for the same reason you don't sell your town house," his mother said. "When was the last time you spent any time there?"

"I stopped by yesterday, as a matter of fact."

He should have thought before he spoke. Lily immediately picked up on the information he'd let slip and said, "I didn't realize that was *your* house."

"You mean to say he took you there?" Natalie exclaimed. "Well, aren't you the lucky one! He's never let me set foot inside the front door."

"Lily didn't, either," he said hurriedly. "I was in and out so fast, it wasn't worth giving her the grand tour. Anyhow, to get back to Hugo's birthday bash, what can I do to help?"

"Show up without Penny Stanford, for a start," his sister replied, dissolving into giggles.

Cynthia smacked her playfully on the wrist with her napkin. "Behave yourself, you wicked child! Lily, how's your lobster?"

She rolled her eyes. "It's wonderful, a real treat. I'm enjoying it thoroughly."

Too thoroughly, he thought, watching her. A minute smudge of melted butter smeared her chin and he itched to reach across the table and wipe it away with his finger.

She caught him staring and laughed. "What's the matter, Sebastian? Do I have dirt on my face?"

"As a matter of fact, you do," he said, irritated with himself, with her, and the whole damned setup. He prided himself on being a take-charge kind of guy and it irked him that she so easily set him off balance. "You've dribbled butter down your chin."

"Sebastian!" His mother looked shocked.

"Well, better she knows and does something about it before it drips on her dress."

"That's the trouble with lobster," Hugo said, ever the peacemaker. "I've always contended the only way to eat it is sitting around a picnic table wearing a bathing suit. That way, a person can be hosed off afterward. Here, Lily, allow me." He blotted her chin with his own napkin. "There you are, good as new."

The rest of the meal progressed without incident. Sebastian kept his eyes to himself, left the others to carry the bulk of the conversation and, when he couldn't avoid responding, confined himself to neutral replies.

As soon as was decently possible, he left the women happily conferring on party arrangements and followed Hugo to his study for an after-dinner drink.

"Well, what do you think of her?" Helping himself to

the one daily cigar his doctor allowed, Hugo settled in his favorite chair and regarded Sebastian curiously.

Weighing the port decanter's heavy crystal stopper on the palm of his hand, Sebastian tossed the question back. "More to the point, what do *you* think of her?"

"I find her very generous. Very willing to forgive."

"She has nothing to be forgiving about, Hugo. You're the one who was betrayed."

"But she doesn't know that. She thinks I walked away from her and left another man to assume my parental responsibilities. In my opinion, Neil Talbot more than proved himself up to the job."

"How did you explain having apparently abandoned her?"

"I didn't." Hugo accepted the glass Sebastian handed to him. "I gave her an abbreviated version of the truth, and told her how deeply I regretted not having exercised my paternal options."

"You have nothing to feel remorseful about, Hugo, and she needs to know that."

"Nevertheless, I've been burdened by guilt for the last twenty-six years." He made a gesture of appeal. "What if Neil had resented being saddled with another man's child? What if he'd deserted Genevieve and she'd fallen on hard times? If she hadn't been able to keep her baby, Lily could have been placed in foster care or adopted by strangers, and lost to me forever."

"Why torture yourself with 'what if's?' None of those things happened."

"But I didn't know that until a few months ago. I didn't even know if Genevieve gave birth to a son or a daughter, and that preyed on my mind a very great deal. No matter how many other good things came into my life, there was always this big empty space where another child should have been.''

"Your whereabouts were never a secret. If things had not gone well for Genevieve, she knew where to find you and you'd have been the first to hear about it.'' He savored a mouthful of the port, before continuing, "At the very least, she'd have come after you for child support. From everything you've told me about her, she was above all else a survivor.''

"Until her luck ran out.'' Hugo inspected the glowing tip of his cigar critically. "I've always appreciated your loyalty, Sebastian. More than anyone else, you've been the one who's comforted me the most when the past came back to haunt me. I've been able to talk to you about things I could never discuss with your mother. But you have to promise me you won't let what you know about Genevieve taint your feelings toward Lily.''

"That's a tall order, given the circumstances. It's not as if you never made an effort to get to know her. How old was she when you tried to make contact—fifteen, sixteen?''

"Just turned fourteen. And remember, I addressed my inquiries to her mother and never did contact Lily directly.''

Sebastian shrugged. "She was old enough to make up her own mind, regardless of any outside pressure that might have been brought to bear on her. And she chose to rebuff your overtures.''

"You're assuming she knew of them, but from what I gathered in our conversation before dinner, clearly she didn't. If you're going to assign blame, Sebastian, then blame me. I could have pursued the matter but I chose not to, and gave up hope of ever getting to know my first born. It's sad that the opportunity to reverse that decision rose out of someone else's tragedy but I'm deeply grateful I've been given another chance.''

"I'm not trying to spoil your reunion, Hugo, but I can't help feeling Lily's turned to you now out of some sort of expediency, and that makes me uneasy. I don't want to see you hurt again.''

"Keep an open mind, Sebastian. You can do that, can't you?''

"Sure,'' he said. "Until she gives me reason to think otherwise, I'll accept the person she appears to be.''

It was as close as he could come to saying what Hugo wanted to hear, without telling an outright lie. But Sebastian remained more determined than ever to have Lily Talbot investigated.

When they emerged from the study an hour later, they found Natalie alone at the table in the breakfast room, a stack of books and a notepad in front of her. "Mother's in the hot tub,'' she told her father.

"And Lily?'' Hugo asked.

"Walking Katie. She said she needed to stretch her legs before she turned in.''

"Then I think I'll join your mother. A bit of aqua therapy might help my back spasms. Sebastian, we'll see you a week from Saturday, if not sooner?''

"Count on it,'' he said. "I'd never miss your birthday, Hugo, you know that.''

He watched his stepfather head back into the house, noticing the slight limp and the way he paced himself carefully, as if every step hurt. "He's in pain.''

"I know it. He'd never have opted out of meeting Lily's flight otherwise.'' Natalie regarded him slyly. "His bad luck was your good fortune, though, wasn't it?''

"How so?''

"You know...you and Lily. *Alone!*''

"What the hell is that supposed to mean?" Surely the woman hadn't spilled the beans about their sharing the same bed the night before? If she had, he'd have her head!

"Oh, come off it, Sebastian! You can hardly keep your eyes off her and you practically come unglued every time she looks back at you."

"I *what?*"

Natalie snickered. "Did you really think I wouldn't notice? I've known you all my life, brother dear, and while I admit I haven't seen it happen often, I recognize the signs. You're smitten."

"You've had too much sun," he told her testily. "It's all I can do to be civil to the woman."

"So I noticed. It's what first tipped me off."

"The little boys you run around with might develop infatuations on the strength of twenty-four hours' acquaintance, Nat, but men my age—!" He stopped and banged the heel of his hand to his forehead. "Why am I defending myself against this absurd accusation?"

"I'm wondering the same thing," she smirked.

He yanked gently on a lock of her hair. "Hit the books, kiddo, and leave the psychoanalysis to the experts. You're way off base with this one."

"You're leaving before Lily gets back from her walk?"

"You bet," he said. "I've seen enough of her for one day."

"Do me a favor before you go." She flipped through her notes and handed him a slip of paper. "See if there's a copy of this book in the library, will you? Dad said he thought there might be."

"Sure."

He headed back into the house and crossed the hall. The library door stood ajar and swung quietly open at his touch. Evening sunlight streamed through the long windows, casting a golden patina over the cherrywood desk, and spotlighting Lily Talbot kneeling before the open door of one of the glass-fronted cabinets under the bookcases.

For a moment he watched her, noting her absorption. Several large leather-bound albums lay on the floor beside her, suggesting she'd been there for some time.

"The last I heard, even dogs as smart as Katie aren't interested in learning to read," he said, finally making his presence known.

She almost jumped out of her skin. Her startled exhalation gusted across the room and the book she'd been inspecting slipped from her hands. "Heavens, you scared me!"

"So it would seem. Exactly what are you doing in here?"

"Looking at old family photos," she said. "Hugo's got pictures going back a hundred and fifty years. There are some of my great-great-grandfather when he was a boy. And look!" She leafed through one of the albums on the floor beside her. "This is one of my great-grandmother when she was about my age. You can see the family resemblance. We have the same shaped face and eyes."

He didn't budge. "You were supposed to be walking the dog. At least, that's the impression you gave Natalie."

"I tried, but Katie was more interested in the river and I wasn't sure it was safe for her to be in the water, so I cut the walk short."

"And decided instead to poke around in here and help yourself to whatever took your fancy. Sneaking through other people's private possessions is practically an Olympic sport with you, isn't it?"

"Hugo gave me permission to look through the family albums whenever I please. How else do you think I knew where to find them? And you're a fine one to talk about being sneaky! I didn't notice you being very forthcoming about the fact that the reason you never invite anyone in the family to visit your town house is that you have your pregnant ladylove holed up there.''

It wasn't often he found himself at a loss for words, but this latest broadside, wide of the mark though it was, left him temporarily speechless. ''My ladylove?'' he finally managed to say.

''*Pregnant* ladylove. Let's not gloss over that small fact.''

Working hard to keep a straight face, he said, ''You mean, you actually deal with fact on occasion—when you're not jumping to wildly inaccurate conclusions, that is?''

''Sneer all you like,'' she spat. ''I know what I saw. All that hugging and kissing, not to mention the length of time you left me twiddling my thumbs while the pair of you...''

She trailed off and gnawed her bottom lip, looking uncertain all at once.

''Well, hell, don't stop now, Lily,'' he said mockingly. ''I can hardly wait to hear the rest.''

''You went upstairs.'' Something fascinating about her left forefinger captured her attention and prevented her from meeting his gaze. ''I saw the bedroom light go on.''

''Pity I didn't leave a ladder strapped to the top of the car. You could have used it to gain a better view of what was going on up there and blackmailed me with what you witnessed.''

She shot him a venomous glare. ''No need to be sarcastic, Sebastian. I assume she's married and that's why you're so reluctant to let anyone in the family know about her. Well, don't worry. Your secret's safe with me.''

''It had better be,'' he said, deciding the game had gone

on long enough, "because the woman you saw is indeed married, although she's not my mistress, nor is that my child she's carrying. She happens to be the friend and client of a colleague, temporarily hiding out from a violent, abusive husband who's already threatened her safety and attempted to flee the country with their three-year-old son. The boy happened to wake up from his nap yesterday while I was there, which no doubt explains why you saw a light go on in an upstairs window. Sorry if that's not colorful enough to satisfy your overactive imagination, but it happens to be the truth."

"Oh," she said, sounding as if she'd had the wind knocked out of her.

He eyed her grimly. "Under no circumstances is what I've told you to leave this room."

"Of course not. And..." She worried her lip again. "I owe you an apology. I'm afraid I accused you unjustly."

"You certainly did," he said, strolling to the reference section to find the book Natalie needed. "Afternoon quickies, crammed in between other appointments, aren't my style at all. Where seduction's concerned, I like to take my time.

Her eyes grew big as saucers and she blushed like a rose. Enjoying her discomfiture, he located the book, then made for the door. "Oh, yes, and one more thing," he said by way of a parting shot. "Contrary to what you might have been brought up to expect, not every woman has the morals of an alley cat and jumps into bed with whichever man happens to take her fancy."

The sky had faded to purple but the heat of the day still lay thick on the air when he finally got back to his apartment. A perfect ending to a less than perfect day, he thought, opening all the windows to the night scent of Hugo's flower gardens.

He still had a briefcase full of notes to go over, a string of phone calls to return and a sluggish lack of enthusiasm for tackling either. Too much good food and wine, on top of more irritation than any one man should have to suffer in a day, and not nearly enough exercise, he decided. What he needed was a long run.

Ignoring the flashing light on his telephone answering machine, he changed into shorts and T-shirt, grabbed a towel and set off down the narrow driveway leading from the stables to the road. Settling into an easy stride, he passed through the gates, turned right and jogged up the shoulder of the hill on the first leg of an arduous five-mile circuit.

Such grueling punishment should have been enough to banish Lily Talbot from his thoughts. With any other woman, it would have been. But the memory of her—the sound of her voice, her disturbingly attractive mouth, the sweep of her glossy hair—went with him, buzzing around in his mind like a mosquito and giving him no peace at all.

Because of her, he was deceiving Hugo, if not overtly then certainly by omission. That alone was reason enough to resent her. That he also found himself fascinated by her merely added to his irritation. She was stylish and carefree and unpredictable. She was everything he didn't want in a woman. Left to her own devices, she'd derail his entire life and everyone else's that he cared about.

He was not a man given to fanciful notions; logic, cause and effect—these were the touchstones by which he pursued his profession. Yet he could not rid himself of the superstitious feeling that she spelled trouble. For what seemed like the hundredth time, Sebastian wished she'd never come into their lives.

Hugo and Cynthia had made an early night of it. Natalie was holed up in her room studying. Save for the grandfather clock chiming eleven in the front hall, the house was silent.

It had been an emotionally exhausting two days and she should have been tired, but after an hour of tossing and turning in bed, Lily gave up on sleep. Too many questions about the past still remained unanswered.

Why had her mother never told her about Hugo? He seemed such a decent man, so eager to welcome her into his family. It was difficult to reconcile that with the fact that he'd never come forward as her father until she searched him out.

When she'd tried asking him why he'd let another man raise her, he'd been evasive. There was something he wasn't telling her; she could feel it in her bones. She sensed, too, that there was a hurt in him that ran very deep.

Flinging back the sheet, she climbed out of bed and went to lean on the sill of the open window beside the desk. At the foot of the garden, the river slid silently past, a ribbon of dark silk in the starlit night. By craning her neck, she could see over the treetops to the roof of the building that Natalie had told her was where Sebastian had his apartment. A light glimmered through the branches, showing he was home.

Everyone around her had a sense of place, of belonging. They all knew where they'd sprung from and where they were headed. Only she was adrift in a sea of uncertainty. Despite her warm welcome here, she remained alone. The sense of connection that came from knowing she belonged just wasn't there yet. Maybe it never would be. Maybe she'd never really feel part of this family.

That she was even here at all was a matter of luck. If she hadn't found among her mother's possessions the envelope containing old photographs, a marriage license and her own birth certificate, she'd never have known Genevieve had been married before or that Neil Talbot wasn't her biological father. Given her happy childhood, it shouldn't have mattered. But it did. The people she'd trusted the most had deceived her.

All at once, the spacious, elegant room was too confining, too suffocatingly hot and humid. Her cotton nightshirt stuck to her skin. She ran a finger inside the neck, suddenly longing for the cool Pacific night air of Vancouver; for the gentle sigh of the sea breeze stirring the branches of the western hemlock tree outside her apartment window.

A flicker of light below and to her right drew her attention to the faint prick of stars reflected on the calm surface of the swimming pool. Inspired, she exchanged the nightshirt for a bathing suit, took a towel from the bathroom and stole through the quiet house to the French doors leading to the back terrace.

Except for a series of mushroom-shaped lights lining the path, the garden lay in darkness—until she rounded the corner to the tiled deck of the pool, that was, when a pair of motion-activated floodlights flared to life and, contrary to what she'd expected, showed that she was not the only one bent on a late-night swim.

A seal-dark head broke the surface of the water and a voice, unmistakably Sebastian's and unmistakably ticked-off, echoed across the pool. "What the hell...! Who's out there?"

"Me," she said, stepping forward. "I came to swim."

"Well, forget it," he snapped. "I got here first."

How like him to think he could chase her off as if she were a common trespasser! "I think it's safe to say the pool's plenty big enough for two."

"I'm willing to bet I can change your mind on that."

She dropped her towel, kicked off her sandals and very deliberately stepped onto the diving board. "I doubt it. I've never been one to back down to a bully."

"Hold it right there, Lily!"

"Why should I?"

With smooth, powerful strokes, he swam to the far end of the pool, the water flashing like diamonds around him. "Because, if you're determined to butt in where you're not wanted, you'll have to get rid of the swimsuit first."

"That's one of the house rules, is it?" she said, her words dripping with sarcasm.

"Tonight it is."

"And why is that, Sebastian?"

"There's an old proverb that goes along the lines of *When in Rome*—"

"*Do as the Romans.* I'm familiar with it, surprising though you might find that."

"Then you ought to be able to figure out why the swimsuit comes off before you come in. You saw last night how I like to get rid of my clothes the first chance I get, Lily. I'm buck naked in here."

Her mother had been a stickler for good manners. *It's impolite to stare* had been one of the first rules of etiquette she'd impressed on her daughter. It wasn't enough to stop Lily's eyes from almost popping out of her head now, though. "You're what?"

"You heard."

"The almighty Sebastian Caine is *skinny-dipping?*"

"That's right. And if you insist on joining me, you're going to be doing the same."

"Forget it! I'm not putting on a one-woman peep show for your entertainment." She jumped back down to the pool deck and scuttled over to where she'd left her towel and sandals.

She moved quickly, but he was even quicker, stroking powerfully across the width of the pool to where she had bent to retrieve her belongings. He grabbed her by the ankle, a move to which she greatly objected. "Chicken!" he taunted.

She squatted down and faced him eyeball to eyeball. His lashes clustered in wet clumps, his hair lay plastered to his skull and his skin gleamed bronze in the unearthly green light of the pool. "If you're so brave, hop out here where I can get a good look at all I'm missing."

He laughed and without warning switched his hold to her wrist and yanked her forward so that she pitched face first into the water. Her limbs tangled with his; flesh slid against flesh, fabric against fabric.

She came up sputtering and furious. "You lied! You *are* wearing swimming trunks!"

"And you," he said, smiling evilly, "were just about wetting yourself in anticipation of discovering otherwise."

She spat out a mouthful of water. "You wish!"

"Uh-huh."

The way he was staring at her mouth disconcerted her more than a little. For no logical reason, a warmth stole through her that had nothing to do with the balmy night. *"What?"* she snapped, when she could bear his scrutiny no longer.

His gaze scoured the rest of her features. "Still trying to figure out what's really going on behind that innocent face.'' He drifted so close that there was scarcely an inch of water separating their bodies. "Come on, Lily," he murmured, persuasive as a lover bent on seduction, "it's just you and me—no one else around to overhear. Tell me what you're really after.''

"I already have," she said, suddenly fighting for breath. He was all rangy, hard muscle; an athlete posing as an officer of the courts. Tanned when he should have been pale and bookish; exciting when he should have been dull and austere. Nearly naked when he ought to have been buttoned up in a three-piece suit and conservative tie.

All right, her heart told her, when her head was insisting he was all wrong!

She tried to back away from him but he forestalled her by bracing both his arms against the side of the pool so that she was imprisoned between them. She tried to *look* away, but his eyes held her captive, their blue flame burning clean through to her soul. "Why won't you believe me?''

"Because I've learned to trust my instincts.'' He leaned closer; so close she could detect on his breath a trace of some sweet, heavy wine—port, perhaps, or apricot brandy—and almost feel the new beard growth stubbling his jaw. "And they tell me you spell nothing but trouble.''

For no good reason at all, she was a mess. Her pulse was fluttering and stalling like a demented butterfly. Her windpipe felt constricted all the way from her lungs to her throat. She didn't know what to do with her hands. If she moved them, she'd make contact with some part of that tanned, toned body hemming her in so effectively. And regardless of how *his* instincts were operating, *hers* were screaming out loud and clear that touching him anywhere would be a very unwise move.

So she sort of hung there in the water, and doing her best to eliminate the silly, adolescent breathiness still plaguing her voice, said, "I hope you like crow because you're going to be eating a lot of it before the summer's over."

He opened his mouth to speak and she cringed inwardly, expecting he'd fire back some pithy retort. Instead their gazes locked and everything around them grew suddenly still, leaving them isolated in a capsule of expectant silence.

Nothing prepared her for what happened next and, afterward, she couldn't have said who took the first step in the agonizingly slow journey that followed. Perhaps neither of them did, and some powerful magnetic current drew them together until their lips were barely touching.

The impact to her senses stunned her. He was so unfeeling in many ways—in his attitude, the things he said to her—that she'd have expected his lips to be cruel. But they settled on hers with such eloquent finesse that she found herself yearning toward him.

At that, the pressure of his mouth increased. His hand meandered down to bracket the indentation of her waist. A thousand sensory pinpoints sprang to life, electrifying the swath of skin grazed by his fingertips. His hips nudged hers, a fleeting contact only, but enough to remind her that what was happening above water had repercussions below the surface.

It was all so unexpected, so foolish, really. They disliked each other. Their short acquaintance was larded with suspicion and wariness. Yet their bodies recognized a rapport their minds refused to acknowledge, and melded with such complete trust that she found herself dangerously close to losing sight of his true objective.

This was not irresistible attraction run wild, nor even rampant lust. It was calculated seduction.

She pulled away just a fraction and met his unblinking gaze. Was it really fire she detected in the depths of his eyes—or the cold blue steel of dedicated hostility?

"Maybe," he said, an unaccustomed hoarseness ruffling his words, "it's time we called an end to this."

"I don't think so," she said. "Not until you explain what you meant by that remark you made earlier tonight, just before you left the library—the one about not all women having the morals of alley cats. Was what happened just now your way of putting the theory to the test?"

CHAPTER FIVE

TO HIS credit, he didn't feign ignorance of what she was referring to, but nor did he give her a straightforward answer. "Never mind. I spoke out of turn," he said, then did a neat underwater flip and swam to the other side of the pool.

Before she'd begun to catch her breath or recover from the devastation of his kiss, he'd climbed out and disappeared along a side path toward the stables, moving so swiftly that she was left to wonder if she'd imagined the whole kissing incident.

That pretty much set the pattern for the days that followed. For the most part, Sebastian avoided having to deal directly with her, which wasn't too difficult since his law office was in town. But for a gainfully employed man, he seemed able to take a lot of time away from his clients to monitor her movements.

One morning, she was busy cutting dead heads from the roses and suddenly got the eerie sense she was being watched. She looked around, found the garden deserted, then caught sight of him spying on her from a window in the house. What did he think, she wondered, half amused, half annoyed. That she planned to steal the best blooms and sell them on the nearest street corner?

Another afternoon so soporific with heat that it was all anyone could do to walk six paces without melting, she and Natalie were fooling around in the pool. The glare on the water was blinding, so when she hauled herself onto the tiled deck and raced to the umbrella table to apply more sunscreen, she didn't notice Sebastian lounging in one of the chairs until she almost tripped over his feet.

"Having a good time?" he inquired, his eyes unreadable behind dark aviator glasses but his tone so frosty she almost shivered. At least, that's how she chose to justify the goose bumps popping out all over her skin, because to admit to the other possibility—that being this close to him brought back too-vivid memories of their last intimate encounter—was not to tolerated.

"Yes," she replied, adopting the confrontational attitude that was becoming almost habitual in her dealings with him. "Does that offend you?"

"When it interferes with my sister's studies, it does. You might have nothing else to do but romp in the sun, but Natalie will be writing final exams in another month and her time would be better occupied studying. In case you haven't heard, her ambitions amount to something a bit more intellectually taxing than arranging flowers."

Lily had a very respectable diploma in horticulture to her credit but, "Natalie is an adult, Sebastian," she told him, choosing to save until another time the news that she was not quite the mental lightweight he perceived her to be. "I doubt she needs you to organize her time or remind her of her priorities. And since she happens to be as much my sister she is yours, you can safely assume I, too, have her best interests at heart."

He whipped off his glasses and subjected her to one of his most imperious stares. It was criminal, she thought, that any man should be blessed with such compellingly beautiful eyes. They put a woman off-kilter, made her forget she was dealing with the enemy and tempted her to dwell on possibilities best left to molder in obscurity. "That kind of sentiment might fool everyone else around here," he said flatly, "but it doesn't wash with me so you might as well save your breath."

The rejection stung worse than a slap on her wet skin, though heaven knew she should be used to it by now. "You want to know your trouble?" she countered, reining in a strong urge to shake her wet hair and drip water all over his immaculately creased dress pants. "You're jealous because you've forgotten how it feels to have fun. That's assuming you ever knew how in the first place, of course! And I'll tell you something else—you're also unnaturally possessive. You think you own Natalie, and it's been a real shock to your system to have someone else usurp her affections."

"Don't flatter yourself, Lily," he sneered. "You happen to be the flavor of the week, that's all."

That he remained so impeccably unruffled by her attack, while she'd worked herself into an outright sweat by his was the only excuse she could offer for what she said next. "Flavor of the week, hmm? So *that's* what you found so irresistible the other night that you simply had to sample it by kissing me!"

He rose languidly to his feet and towered over her. "I kissed you to relieve the tedium of your incessant chatter, but it's not a mistake I intend to repeat. Go back to your girlish games with my sister, cupcake. You're out of your league trying to match wits with me."

"And what are you going to do to pass the time, Sebastian? Continue to play the part of my personal prison warden?"

"I don't know what you're talking about."

"Of course you do! Or did you think I haven't noticed the way you're always lurking in the bushes like some third-rate undercover agent waiting to catch me in some unspeakable act of espionage?"

"Good God!" he said, a small smile curling his mouth. "I had no idea you numbered paranoia among your other dubious qualities. Thank you for drawing it to my attention."

Having once again had the last word, he brushed off his hands and sauntered away.

And so it went for nearly two weeks: parry and thrust, every time their paths happened to cross. By the morning of Hugo's birthday, she was ready to weep with frustration at Sebastian's unremitting antipathy toward her, and almost dreaded that night's party for fear of how he might try to humiliate her in front of the guests.

She could only hope he'd have eyes for no one but his date, Penny Stanford. When she confided as much to her sister, though, as they worked on the flower decorations, Natalie declared rather ambiguously, "Sebastian might like to pretend that'll be the case but if you ask me, his eyes have been wandering of late and it's my bet someone else has become the object of his affections."

Unwilling to admit that the unpleasant lurch of her stomach could possibly be ascribed to dismay, Lily made a minor adjustment to one of the floral arrangements and said with studied indifference, "Really? Anyone I know?"

Natalie stifled a giggle. "Oh, yes—better than anybody, if you get my drift! But I've already said too much and Sebastian would throttle me if he knew I'd even brought the subject up. He's a very private individual, you know."

"*Secretive's* the word I'd use."

Natalie looked at her curiously. "Don't you like him, Lily?"

The question was simple enough; the answer unexpectedly complex.

Did she? Too much, perhaps, despite their frequent run-ins? And was the feeling mutual? Was the reason they worked so hard at insulting each other nothing but a defense mechanism designed to prevent them from facing up to underlying feelings neither was brave enough to acknowledge? If so, how adolescent!

"I'm not sure," she finally said. "He's a difficult person to read and he's seemed resentful of me from the first."

"It's because of the way your mother treated my—" Natalie began, then turned bright red and clapped her hand to her mouth. "Oh, sorry, Lily! I shouldn't have said that."

Lily's heart gave a peculiar jolt. Hugo had changed the subject when she'd tried to ask him about her mother, Sebastian had clammed up, and now Natalie was behaving as if she'd dragged some horrendous skeleton out of the closet by mentioning Genevieve's name. "Perhaps you shouldn't have, but now that you've started, I wish you'd finish."

"I can't. I promised Dad." She made a big production of checking her watch. "Heavens, look at the time! Eleven o'clock already. Mom and Dad'll be back from the golf club soon, and we haven't even begun on the table decorations! You get started on them and I'll go cut more sweet peas."

Puzzled, Lily watched her leave. What did they all know—or think they knew—that they couldn't share with her?

"Sometimes, marriages fail, especially the May-December kind like mine and Genevieve's," was all Hugo would admit, whenever she pressed him to talk about the past. "There was some bitterness, we parted and I elected to forfeit my right to know my child. It wasn't a wise choice but, at the time, it seemed the best choice.

Enough to say, my dear Lily, that I have lived with the guilt of that decision ever since and welcome this chance to make up for my omission. Let's leave it at that and go forward from here.''

Easy for him to say, when he already had all the answers, but impossible for her! Sometimes, she wished she'd never found out that Neil wasn't her biological father. Just when she was beginning to come to terms with her parents' death, her life had been thrown into turmoil yet again, and she hadn't known a moment's real peace since.

Well, no more! The truth was supposed to set a person free and before the day was ended, she intended to find release from her particular prison.

She waded in as soon as Natalie returned with the sweet peas. ''You know, Natalie, I'd never ask you to betray a confidence, so perhaps you aren't free to talk about my mother, but there's nothing to stop me from telling you what *I* know about her.''

''I wish you wouldn't. I wish you'd forget I ever mentioned her name.''

''I can't. She doesn't deserve to be swept aside like this, as if she were never of any consequence.'' She touched her sister's arm pleadingly. ''She was a wonderful wife and a wonderful mother. I never came home from school to an empty house, the way some children do. She was always there, eager to hear about my day, and always ready to welcome my friends. She made our home a place that was full of love and warmth and laughter, and it hurts me that no one here thinks well of her.''

Natalie plucked at the sweet pea stems uncertainly. ''People aren't always what they seem, Lily.''

''I know that. Why else do you think I contacted Hugo this last May? Because there was an important part of my mother's life that I knew nothing about. I *had* to fill in the blanks.''

"But don't you see, there's a problem right there? Your parents died last September, yet you waited eight months before you decided to get in touch with Dad. If it was that important to learn what happened, why didn't you come to him sooner?''

"Because I didn't know he was my father until after the estate was settled, and probating a will takes months. As soon as it was complete, I had access to the safe-deposit box my parents had leased from the bank that looked after their financial affairs, and that's when I found the envelope.''

She drew in a steadying breath as she recalled that fateful morning. "I never expected it would be easy, finalizing the last details, but at first it didn't seem so bad. Money is nothing more than figures printed on a statement and can't really hurt a person. Even cash possesses a sort of cold impersonality, having already passed through thousands of strangers' hands before touching ours. But the safe-deposit box...''

"If this is too difficult for you, you don't have to go on.''

"Yes, I do! I have to make you understand that I need to find closure before I can get on with my life.'' Determined to finish what she'd started, Lily blinked furiously to stem the threatening tears. But the same wave of painful nostalgia that had assailed her when she'd opened the box swept over her again as she relived the moment.

"The little velvet bags protecting my mother's more valuable pieces of jewelry retained traces of her perfume, Natalie. One of her fine blond hairs was tangled in the clasp of a gold chain. A cameo locket held miniatures of her and Neil. Their signatures were scrawled on various documents—the deed to their house, a copy of their will, a life insurance policy. It was as if my mother and father were suddenly standing there beside me, encouraging me to go on. I felt their presence so strongly, it was... unnerving. Uncanny.''

She stopped and pressed a hand to her trembling mouth for a moment. ''Then I found the envelope, hidden under everything else at the very bottom of the box, and learned that Neil wasn't my father at all, nor was he my mother's first husband. And I felt betrayed by the people I loved the most.''

''Was it a letter to you?'' Natalie's voice was hushed with sympathy.

Somehow, Lily managed a laugh. ''If only it had been, I might not be pleading my case with you now. But no, there was nothing addressed to me personally. I found a photograph of my mother. She looked very young, but I recognized her immediately. She was wearing a wedding outfit—very formal, all lace and satin, with a train and a veil and everything—and was on the arm of a man a good bit older. He wore a morning suit and I realize now that he was Hugo. There was a photographer's inscription on the back—*Mr. and Mrs. Hugo Preston, Stentonbridge, Ontario,* and the date—two years before I was born.''

''And that's all you found?''

''No. There was a copy of an early birth certificate of mine, naming Hugo Preston as my father, also my mother and Neil's marriage certificate, dated when I was eleven months old, and last, adoption papers making Neil Talbot my legal father.''

She faced Natalie again. ''And that was it. So you see why I came here looking for more information. I know all the 'whats,' but none of the 'whys.' ''

"I can't help you," Natalie said. "I wish I could. For a start, I don't have the complete picture, only bits and pieces I've picked up at one time or another. I'm afraid that if Dad won't tell you what you want to know, the only other person you can turn to is Sebastian. He knows the whole story."

"And flatly refuses to discuss it with me." She slumped into a chair at the table. "I don't know where else to turn."

Natalie took a seat across from her. "What if I were to ask Sebastian to talk to you?"

"I doubt he'd listen," she said miserably.

"He might. It's worth a try." Natalie nibbled thoughtfully on her lip for a moment, then slapped the flat of her hand on the tabletop. "I'm going to do it! This afternoon!"

"You'll never pull it off."

"Watch me! Sebastian's basically a very fair man, and I think I can convince him you deserve to know your own history. You're going to have to strike while the iron's hot, though, before he's had time to change his mind, and that means finding some reason to pry him loose from Penny at the party, and getting him by himself, because you know this isn't something he'll discuss in front of a crowd. Oh, yes, and one more thing, Lily." She leaned forward and cupped her mouth close to Lily's ear. "Try buttering him up a bit between now and then, if you get the chance, instead of baiting him all the time. It might make my end of the job that much easier to pull off."

A figure moved out of the shadows on the terrace and into the sunlight flooding through the open French doors. "What's all the whispering about?" Sebastian wanted to know. "I thought the pair of you were supposed to be working on the flowers for tonight?"

A guilty flush swept over Natalie's face. "Oh, we were just…talking."

He eyed her suspiciously, then swung his attention to Lily. "Were you badgering my sister? Is that why she's twitching like a nervous cat?"

Natalie, bless her heart, sprang to Lily's defense. "Stop picking on her, Sebastian! I'm her sister, too, and she wasn't badgering me at all. She was telling me how sweet you were to her the night the road was washed out and you ended up in that awful motel."

Briefly he seemed at a loss for words—a remarkable occurrence, in Lily's experience of the man—but not entirely surprising. She was pretty taken aback herself, given that she'd said almost nothing to anyone about that particular evening. But then she caught the meaningful *butter-him-up* stare Natalie directed at her behind Sebastian's back, and tried to pick up her cue. "Yes," she said brightly. "Exactly."

If anything, he looked more dubious than ever, but before he could pursue the subject, the swish of tires on gravel alerted them to Hugo and Cynthia's return from their early-morning round of golf. A moment later, their voices could be heard as they came around the side of the house.

"Never mind that rubbish. Let's get this job done and out of the way before the caterers arrive." Reasserting control, Sebastian swept up an urn containing a massive arrangement of white gladioli. "Lily, tell me where to put this."

Oh, don't tempt me, Sebastian Caine! she thought. *You wouldn't like my answer!*

He bathed her in a Machiavellian smile. "I just read your thoughts, honey, and they weren't pretty."

She was ready to kick him where it would hurt the

most. To tell him that he was the most arrogant, controlling creature ever to cross her path and that she hated him. *Hated him!* Except it wasn't true. And pretending otherwise wasn't helping her cause any.

Taking a deep breath, she made a sincere effort to banish the antagonism that kept coming between them. "Please let's stop this senseless sparring, Sebastian, and at least try to get along."

"Why?"

"For Hugo, and your mother, if nothing else. I think they'd like us to be friends."

"So what you're suggesting is just for their sakes and has nothing to do with your personal agenda?"

"What are you implying?" She attempted a laugh that came out sounding more like a nervous whinny. "That I harbor a secret fondness for you?"

He looked at her long and searchingly. "Do you?"

Confronted so directly, she hardly knew where to look or how to answer. That he'd detected something she thought she'd kept well hidden left her feeling slightly queasy. "Put the gladioli on the piano," she mumbled, "and don't ask silly questions."

If giving the party a miss had been an option, he'd have taken it. So, once the birthday toasts were over and the dancing heated up, Sebastian put himself at a safe distance on the fringes of the crowd scattered over the lower lawn.

Nursing a glass of champagne, he chatted with Forbes Maynard, the other retired senior partner of the law firm along with Hugo, and tried to keep his attention away from the woman who seemed bent on creating nothing but havoc in everyone's lives.

Even if Forbes hadn't been teetering on the brink of senility, though, she'd have been difficult to ignore. The transformation from working woman in shorts and a T-shirt, with a smudge of dirt on her cheek and her hair tied back in an elastic band, to sought-after belle of the ball, was, to put it bluntly, nothing short of breathtaking.

She wore purple—the kind associated with violets or pansies. Deep and rich and sensual. The neckline fell from narrow shoulder straps to a low vee in front and just about to her waist in the back. The hem swept her ankles. The parts in between were…awe-inspiring.

A pendant on a gold chain nestled just below her throat, with matching earrings suspended from her ears. Though no gemologist, Sebastian knew enough to appreciate the fine quality of the cabochon amethysts pavéd with diamonds, and the hunk of gold on her wrist. Somebody had invested a lot of money in her trinkets. A lover, perhaps? Or was she her own biggest fan?

His thoughts veered to the preliminary report he'd received on her just the day before. *Born to Genevieve and Hugo Preston, August 5. Name changed by adoption to Talbot, July 27. Never married, no known relationships of any significance. Holds annual lease on penthouse in small, older apartment building in West End of Vancouver. Has resided at present address for six years. Drives three-year-old minivan registered to Lily's Flower Nook.*

It had not read like the résumé of a big spender, nor did it give the impression there was a rich boyfriend waiting in the wings. The last surprised him, given the amount of attention she was attracting tonight. When she wasn't charming the women or wowing the old men, she was dancing with younger guys, too many of whom his mother had found to keep her entertained and who were clustered around her as eagerly as flies around a honey jar.

The sight was enough to sour his champagne to vinegar.

But even though they held her in their arms and their eyes damn near popped out of their heads as they tried to get a look down the front of her dress, they didn't know what he knew: that the skin around her waist was taut and satin smooth; or that he'd made her tremble when he'd kissed her, and her eyes had turned huge and dark.

"You were saying, Sebastian?" Forbes was regarding him expectantly.

"Huh?" Feeling as dazed as if he'd walked into a brick wall, Sebastian turned to his companion and struggled to recapture the thread of the conversation.

He'd have had more luck finding a blade of grass in a desert and Forbes seemed to realize it, too. Looking over his shoulder, he followed Sebastian's gaze which, like a magnet attracted to true north, had again fastened on Lily. "Ah, yes," he murmured. "She does tend to make everything else forgettable, doesn't she? I take it she's the long-lost daughter?"

"Uh-huh." He sounded as if he was choking, which he damn near was! *Where the devil did she find that dress? And who sewed her into it? Or had it been sprayed on?*

"Fine-looking woman, wouldn't you say?"

"I guess."

"Looks to me as if she's headed this way." As though sensing he was ready to bolt, Forbes clamped an age-spotted hand over his arm. "Introduce me, Sebastian. I'd like to meet her."

Meet her, my ass! You want to ogle her, you lecherous old goat!

She swayed down the terrace steps and across the lawn, the stuff her dress was made of shimmying over her body like a live thing. The skirt had a mile-high slit up the front, which bared a good three inches of thigh with each step she took. By itself, that was enough to send the fittest man into cardiac arrest and Forbes, who didn't get nearly enough exercise, began panting asthmatically.

A waiter offered her a glass of champagne. Hugo waylaid her and made some remark that had her tipping her head back in laughter. She moved among the guests, looking thoroughly at ease, as if she'd been born to the high life and hadn't a care in the world.

Eventually—unavoidably—she came to where he waited with Forbes hyperventilating at his side. "Hello, Sebastian," she burbled, all smiling, deceptive sweetness. "I don't see any sign of Penny. What happened? Did she stand you up?"

"She had to work."

"Even today?" She fluttered her ridiculous eyelashes in patent disbelief.

"Penny's a nurse, remember?" he said. "Unlike you, she doesn't have the luxury of keeping shop girls' hours. Forbes, this is Lily Talbot, Hugo's daughter from a former marriage."

"Nothing wrong with shop girls," Forbes wheezed, his handshake straying until he was mauling her wrist like a mangy old lion gone too long without a decent meal. "I'm the Maynard in Preston, Maynard, Hearst and Caine, my dear. Too old to be of much value around the office these days, I'm afraid, but not so far gone that I don't appreciate a pretty face."

Extracting herself from his clutches, she bathed him in a smile that left him drooling. "So nice to meet you, Mr. Maynard, and I'd love to chat some time, but right now," she cooed, latching onto Sebastian and maneuvering him toward the terrace, "this man owes me a dance. Remember you promised me, Sebastian?"

"I did no such thing," he growled, but there was no real bite behind his answer. His senses were too clouded by her nearness. How was it that she was fooling everyone but him, yet he was the one falling deepest under her spell?

Her hand felt tiny and fragile wrapped in his. Her hair, piled in gleaming curls on top of her head, brushed his chin. Her perfume teased his nostrils.

Turning into the circle of his arm and fitting her steps perfectly to his, she lifted her face up to his. "If I didn't know better, I'd think you've been avoiding me."

"Given the amount of attention you've been lapping up from just about every other man present, I'm surprised you've had time to notice anything but the success of your debut into local society."

She smiled delightedly at him from under heavy lashes. "Why, Sebastian, you almost sound jealous."

"Surprised, perhaps, that you're causing such a stir, but *jealous?* Don't be ridiculous!"

In fact, he wasn't surprised at all. When he'd first met her, he'd thought her pretty enough in an ordinary sort of way, but not exactly the kind to stop traffic. Maybe the sensible denim skirt and plain white blouse she'd been wearing had fooled him because the truth was, she had a surreptitious glamour that crept up on a man and blind-sided him when he least expected it.

What other reason could there be for him to find himself repeatedly drawn to her when every neuron he possessed warned him to steer clear? How come he could dance the night away with Penny and manage to control his libido until they were alone, but he couldn't hold Lily Talbot's hand for five seconds without getting steamed up?

Good thing the evening had faded to night and shadows as purple as her dress swirled around them. If he couldn't help making a public fool of himself, at least she was the only one who had to know about it.

Driven to test the waters even further despite himself, he inched her a little closer, half expecting she'd kick him in the shin for his nerve. Instead she slid her hand up the lapel of his jacket until her fingers were touching the back of his neck.

"Sebastian?" she murmured, tilting her head so that her lips almost brushed his throat and her breath sifted over him as sweetly as a magnolia-scented breeze. "I guess you know why I dragged you away from Mr. Forbes?"

He heard invitation, sweet and simple, in the way she uttered his name. Thoroughly fired up, he folded her hand against his chest and seized the moment. "Because you wanted to be alone with me?"

"Exactly."

"Then what say we slip away and continue this someplace else?"

She tilted one shoulder provocatively. "I was hoping you'd say that. Where do you suggest we go?"

His better judgment blown to smithereens, he allowed his hand to wander past the low back of her dress and caress the silk-clad curve of her hip. Her mouth, he decided fuzzily, had the texture of a rose; soft, beautiful, easily bruised. "My apartment?" he croaked, barely able to hear himself speak over the drumming of his blood.

"If you like. But a quiet corner of the garden will do just as well." She pulled away slightly, just enough to captivate him with a dark, alluring gaze from beneath the sweep of her lashes. "Anywhere, as long as we aren't disturbed."

He looked over to where Hugo and his mother circulated among their friends, with Natalie, looking somewhat trapped, in tow. "You're not concerned you might be missed?"

"It won't take long." She squeezed his fingers persuasively. "We'll be back before anyone realizes we're gone."

He swallowed. The women he knew were usually more bashful and he wasn't quite sure how to handle such a bold approach. But she was Genevieve Talbot's daughter, after all. Still, "You're sure about this, Lily?" he asked.

She subjected him to another slow, seductive blink. "Absolutely."

"No regrets when it's too late to change things?"

She shook her head. "Not a chance."

Her reassurances notwithstanding, a better man might have had the gumption to decline so willing an invitation. But the simmering attraction between them had risen to the point that he was prepared to postpone dealing with his shortcomings until another time. "Then come with me."

Grasping her hand more securely, he pulled her to the edge of the terrace and around the side of the house to the shortcut that led to his apartment. She might be anticipating nothing more than a quick roll in the hay, but he prided himself on knowing how to prolong a woman's pleasure.

Lily Talbot was in for the surprise of her life.

CHAPTER SIX

FOR a man who had shown marked reluctance every other time she'd broached the subject of her birth, Sebastian was in a tearing hurry to talk to her about it all of a sudden. "Could we slow down, do you think?" she panted, almost tripping as one of her high heels caught between the paving stones.

He turned a glance on her which, even by moonlight, seemed to smolder. "Changing your mind already, Lily?"

"I've never been more sure of anything in my life." She shook her head decisively and glanced around. They'd passed through the rose garden and the shrubbery separating the stables from the main house, and were now so completely beyond the perimeter of the party that even the music was barely audible. "But we're safe enough here, surely? No one's going to overhear us."

A tiny frown creased his forehead. "I should hope not! But to be on the safe side, I'd prefer the privacy of my apartment."

"All right." She shrugged. "Just bear in mind I'm not wearing running shoes, though, will you?"

"Sorry. I wasn't thinking." To her surprise, he clasped her hand warmly, and led her the rest of the way as carefully as if she were made of glass. "Better?"

It was better than better! She liked this more chivalrous side of him; liked having him touch her, just as, when they were dancing, she'd liked the strength of his arm at her back and the almost intimate way he'd held her. Under different circumstances, she'd have savored such a rare occurrence and even have thought he was not unmoved, either, because, once or twice, when his hips had accidentally brushed against hers, she'd thought he was...well, *physically affected*....

But no! Given his manifest dislike of her, she had to have been mistaken. The only possible reason he'd held her close had been to avoid having other people bump into them.

Placing his hand in the small of her back now, he guided her inside the stables, through a door and up a winding staircase to his apartment, a spacious, charming area of vaulted whitewashed ceilings supported by dark cross beams, plain white walls displaying a few very good watercolors, and pegged oak floors scattered with jewel-toned Oriental rugs. The living-room sofas were of black leather, deep and luxurious, the tables, desk and tall armoire antique English cherrywood.

A wall sconce on the landing lent a subdued glow to one end of the long room, but most of the radiance came from the opposite side where bands of moonlight speared a wall of open windows bare of any kind of drapery or blinds. "I had no idea you enjoyed such a splendid view of the river," she said, leaning over the broad sill and inhaling the mingled scents of summer. "You're much closer to the water here than we are in the main house."

"And far enough away from the main house to ensure total privacy."

She heard the rustle of fabric, the sound of him moving around the room, the faint creak of the armoire doors being pulled open. Moments later, the mellow tones of a clarinet seducing the night fused with the musical clink of crystal.

"How about a glass of wine?" he suggested. "I don't have any champagne chilling, but I've got just about anything else, including a very respectable sparkling burgundy.''

She turned to find him watching her intently and, despite the music, the room all at once seemed filled with a taut, waiting silence that left her feeling inexplicably uneasy. That he'd shed his jacket, pulled his bow tie loose and undone the top button of his dress shirt, didn't help. It served as too vivid a reminder of how casually he'd climbed out of his clothes that night in the motel, and had her wondering, irrationally, if he was planning a repeat performance now.

Swallowing to relieve her dry mouth, she said, ''I'd just as soon get straight down to business, if you don't mind.''

For the first time since she'd known him, he looked thoroughly disconcerted. Shoving his hands into his pockets, he took a turn across the room and back again, then swung to a stop in front of her. ''I like a woman who knows what she wants, Lily, make no mistake about that,'' he finally said, ''but I confess I'm not keen on one who's in such a hurry to get to the main event that she can't be bothered with a little foreplay, even if it's only the social kind.''

She stared at him, stunned. ''I don't think I heard you correctly. Did you say *foreplay?*''

''I did.'' He closed the distance between them and hooked a finger under the shoulder strap of her gown. ''What would you like to call it?''

''I...I...!'' Realizing her mouth was hanging open, she snapped it closed and blinked. ''I didn't realize straightforward communication required any sort of...*preliminaries!*''

''You prefer to hoist up your skirt and just get on with it, do you?'' He stroked the side of her neck lightly. ''No lingering over the finer points of seduction?''

If she'd confounded him moments earlier, his reply reduced her to utter bewilderment now. "Are you drunk?" she asked nervously, edging away from him and wishing suddenly that she'd insisted they remain in the garden.

He tracked her movement with eyes far too clear and observant for him to latch on to *that* as an excuse for his bizarre behavior. Nor did he try. "I'm beginning to wish I was," he replied, barring her way with one arm braced against the wall. "Exactly what is it you want of me, Lily?"

"What I've always wanted from the first—information about my birth. What did you think I wanted?" Then, seeing the disbelief on his face dissolve into ironic amusement, which he tried to hide by shielding his mouth with his other hand, the disjointed parts of their conversation over the last half hour came together in an interpretation entirely different from the one she'd originally understood. "Oh, my stars, you thought I wanted *you?*"

He looked at her from hooded eyes. "The thought did cross my mind, particularly in light of the way you came on to me."

"*Came on—?* I did no such thing!"

"I think I can be forgiven for believing otherwise." His voice dropped to a mocking whisper. *"I was hoping we could slip away from here, Sebastian...anywhere, as long we're alone and won't be disturbed...."*

"I was referring to our not being overheard by anyone else."

"Well, the next time, don't preface the remark by rubbing up against a man until he's ready to explode. And you can wipe that appalled expression off your face. It's a bit late in the day for a woman your age to pretend you don't know what I'm talking about."

"I didn't! I had no idea...!" She stopped, and bit her

lip, ashamed. Hadn't she entertained the suspicion, however briefly, that when they were dancing, he was *enjoying* having her in his arms? "A lot of people like dancing close. It has more to do with...with *style,* than sex."

He let out an exclamation of disgust and strode to the armoire. In seconds, the music came to an end and one of the doors slammed shut. Reaching inside the other, he pulled out a bottle of brandy and splashed an inch into a cut-glass snifter. "Just as a matter of interest, what made you think I'd break down tonight and give you information I've repeatedly refused to divulge every other time you've brought up the subject?"

"Natalie promised she'd talk to you this afternoon, and try to convince you to change your mind. So, when you suggested we leave the party, I naturally assumed she'd succeeded since it obviously isn't something either of us would discuss in front of other people."

He regarded her over the rim of his glass and took a sip of the brandy.

Dismayed by his silence, she tugged nervously at the shoulder strap he'd dislodged. "She didn't get in touch with you, did she?"

"She did not, although she tried several times. I just never got around to returning her calls." His mouth tightened in annoyance. "Not that it would have mattered, anyway, because I've already made it very clear I won't tell you what you want to know, and you had no right asking my sister to intercede on your behalf."

"Perhaps," she said testily, "it's time *I* made a few things clear to you, the first being that I won't allow you to go on dictating my actions. I didn't come here to be given the runaround, and I'm frankly tired of being told to butt out of something which, by any sane person's def-

inition, is most definitely my business. I resent your attitude. I'm not the bad guy here, Sebastian.''

"Nor is Hugo.''

"Perhaps not. But if you continue holding to your code
of silence, you leave me no choice but to go to him again,
and this time I'll insist he answer all my questions, even
though I know the fact that he more or less abandoned
me as a baby is painful for him to relive.''

"And if he refuses to accommodate you?''

"I'll be out of here within the hour and none of you
will ever see or hear from me again.''

She was bluffing, of course, and felt sure he knew it.
Blood ties, however tenuous, were not so easily severed,
and she could no more walk out of Hugo and Natalie's
lives than she could forget her own name.

Surprisingly, though, Sebastian appeared to take her at
her word. "That would kill him.''

"It's a risk I'm prepared to take.''

He swirled the contents of his glass meditatively, then
pinned her in one of his famous legal-eagle stares. "Okay,
I'll make you a deal. I'll tell you what you want to know,
if you'll answer a question for me, first.''

"Ask away,'' she said, dismissing the tremor of unease
that spiraled through her as nothing more than anticipation
at finally achieving her goal. "I've got nothing to lose
and everything to gain.''

"If you believe that, you're in for a nasty surprise.''

He sounded almost sorry for her, but she wasn't about
to be sidetracked by cheap displays of concern at this
point. "Get on with it, Sebastian. What's your question?''

"Have you never asked yourself why your mother
chose to keep you in the dark about events surrounding
your birth? Did it ever occur to you that the reason might
be that she didn't want you to know?''

"That's two questions, but I won't quibble over trifles since the answer in both cases is, no. Mom and I were very close. There was nothing we couldn't share. I think she was simply waiting for the right time to confide in me."

"You're twenty-six years old, Lily. I doubt there was ever going to be a right time."

"You didn't know my mother."

"And you're quite sure you did?"

"Positive."

He paced to the window and stared out. "What would you say if I told you she was an adulteress who had an affair with her obstetrician and left your father before you were born so that she could be with her lover?"

Another tremor, stronger than the first, shook Lily but she stood her ground. "I'd say you were lying. My mother would never do such a thing."

Still with his back toward her, he said, "I'm telling you the truth. Genevieve Preston ran away with her doctor— Neil Talbot, the man you thought was your father—and left behind a husband who adored her. She stole his child, she humiliated him before the entire town, she broke his heart. And if that wasn't enough, she asked him not to pursue his right to know you after you were born."

"I don't believe you! No man worth his salt would agree to such a demand."

"Hugo did, because he was too proud to beg, and because he sincerely believed you'd be better off not being torn between parents who lived at opposite ends of the country."

"He didn't have to agree to that. He could have insisted on his rights."

"He could have ruined Neil Talbot. Do you know what happens to doctors who abuse their positions of authority and trust? They're stripped of their right to practice medicine. Left without the means to earn a decent living. Disgraced in the eyes of society. If I, as a lawyer, were to behave as your adoptive father did, I'd be disbarred. And I can promise you, if ever I were treated as Hugo was, I'd destroy the man who stole my wife and child, not let him leave me the laughingstock of the area. He'd live to regret messing around with what's mine.''

"Because you're arrogant and vindictive!" she cried, her insides churning. "And if Hugo really did as you're suggesting, and made no attempt to enforce his paternal rights, *he* was weak and undeserving!"

In two strides Sebastian was at her side. His eyes were cold, his fingers around her upper arm iron-hard. "He was the best thing that ever happened to Genevieve Talbot! Before she married him, she was nothing. *Nothing,* do you hear? *Trailer trash!* Slinging hamburgers in a truck stop by day, and hanging around bars at night, offering God only knows what in exchange for the price of a drink."

Lily's bid to laugh in his face emerged as high-pitched and devoid of amusement as a crow's dying screech. "Now I know you're lying, because if she was all those things, how did she ever meet such a fine, upstanding pillar of the community as Hugo Preston?"

"A police officer friend of his talked him into representing her when she filed assault charges against one of her barfly associates. Seems that even battered and bruised, she made a beautiful victim. Even though Hugo was twice her age, he fell head over heels in love and married her. It's a familiar enough story—wealthy, sophisticated older man rescues helpless young woman from the wrong side of the tracks, and gives her a better life. But instead of repaying him with loyalty, she dumped him two years later for her young stud of a doctor." He tossed back the rest of his drink and swiped the back of his hand across his mouth. "Once a slut, always a slut, I guess."

Lily had never hit anyone in her life; never been hit, either, come to that. Her mother couldn't abide violence in any form. But at Sebastian's last remark, she lifted her hand and landed it flat across his cheek in a stinging slap. The noise cracked the night like a rifle shot.

He didn't flinch. Showed no reaction at all, in fact. He merely continued to hold her glance and said quietly, "That won't change the truth, Lily."

"It has to," she quavered, clinging desperately to beliefs suddenly and shockingly undermined by facts that made a hideous kind of sense. "You're mistaken. It was never like that."

"It was exactly like that. But you don't have to take my word. There's plenty of other evidence. The letter she left behind when she ran away, the others she wrote when she wanted Hugo to agree to a divorce and give his permission for Talbot to legally adopt you. It's all there in black-and-white, with her name signed at the bottom."

"No! You're protecting Hugo. The truth is, he didn't want to be bothered with a child at his age, and that's why my mother left him."

But she was grasping at straws, and even if she hadn't been willing to admit it, Sebastian wasted no time setting her straight. "If that was the case, why, when he married *my* mother four years later, did he not take steps to prevent Natalie's being conceived? And why, for pity's sake, did he take on a stepson who, at twelve, showed every sign of being a royal pain in the rear as a teenager?"

She twisted her face away, beset by the conclusions crowding her mind. Little things she'd taken for granted as part and parcel of her mother's personality suddenly took on new and painful significance. *Genevieve had*

never touched a drop of liquor; had detested overindul-
gence in others. She'd volunteered her time at a shelter
for battered women. She'd insisted on Lily's attending
college because she herself had never finished high school
and the lack of formal education had cost her dearly when
she was young. She'd displayed a compulsive need to bet-
ter herself, taking one night class course after another
until she'd accumulated enough postsecondary credits to
earn a degree in fine arts.

"Well?" Sebastian continued regarding her patiently.
"Why did Hugo take on another man's family, Lily?"

"I don't know," she said, turning aside her face to hide
her brimming eyes, "and I don't care. I just want to know
why he didn't fight to keep me."

Sebastian cupped her cheek and forced her to look at
him. "He made a mistake. He let hurt pride dictate his
actions and by the time he came to his senses, you thought
Neil Talbot was your father. He loved you enough then
to give you up, and he loves you enough now not to want
to tarnish your memories of your mother by telling you
how things really stood."

"My mother!" she wept bitterly, the truth sweeping
over her in huge, unforgiving waves. "Genevieve Talbot,
the elegant, gracious doctor's wife. The accomplished
hostess. The morally upright citizen whose whole life was
built on a lie. And I believed every word that came out
of her mouth. How that must have amused her!"

Hearing the rising hysteria in her voice, he put his arms
around her and drew her firmly to him, even though she
tried to fight him off. "Don't," he murmured, his hands
stroking in long, strong, comforting sweeps up and down
her spine. "Don't beat yourself up like this. You were the
innocent victim caught in the middle. None of this is your
fault."

"No," she sobbed, beside herself, "it's yours. Oh, I hate you, Sebastian Caine, for what you've taken away from me tonight!"

"I hate myself," he said grimly. "I wish to God I'd kept quiet about what I know. Lily, honey, please don't cry like this. You'll make yourself ill."

"I don't care!" She lifted her tear-ravaged face to his. "Do you know how empty I feel inside? How *ugly?*"

"You're not ugly," he insisted, holding her face in his hands. His voice dropped a notch, took on a husky edge that rendered it almost tender. "You're beautiful and desirable and…!"

And then he was kissing her, his mouth coming down on hers as masterfully as though, by the sheer force of his will, he thought he could undo all the pain he'd brought to her. Kissing her with a dedication and passion so fierce that it kindled a tiny flame in the cold, empty wasteland that seemed to fill her.

She felt his hand at her throat, at her shoulder. Touched her fingertips to his chest and found the rapid, uneven thunder of his heartbeat. Saw, just before her own fell closed, the smoldering heat in his eyes. And the flame grew; flickered and strengthened into a blazing torch radiating through her blood to chase away the chilling horror of the last few minutes.

As quickly as they'd surfaced, all the ghastly details he'd disclosed shriveled in its heat and left behind a rapacious need to *belong*. To be possessed and cherished as if she were the only woman of any consequence left on earth. She wanted to be loved, honestly and without reservation or secrets, if not forever, then at least for a little while.

Her hands roamed the starched front of his shirt,

searched out the pearl studs holding it closed, and tugged them loose with feverish impatience.

He caught her fingers in his, crushed them gently to his bare chest. "This isn't a good time to give in to impulse. Neither of us is thinking straight."

"I don't want to think. I want to feel...to heal." She kissed his throat softly and finished on a sigh, "Help me to do that, Sebastian."

"Be careful you don't start something you're not prepared to finish," he muttered, then floundered into a groan when, undaunted, she dipped her head and circled the tiny bud of his left nipple with her tongue.

"Make love to me," she begged against his skin.

His breath caught in a harsh, agonized rasp. "You didn't want that earlier."

"I want it now," she told him, bisecting the line of dark hair arrowing into the waist of his trousers with the tip of her fingernail.

"It won't make the truth about the past any less ugly."

"This isn't about the past, it's about the here and now. About me—" she skimmed her fingers over his flat, hard belly; toyed with the straining fabric of his fly "—and you."

"Li...ly...!" Her name hovered on the labored whisper of a man fighting a hopeless battle against overwhelming odds.

She swirled her tongue in the hollow of his throat. Massaged the heel of her hand against the rigid contours he couldn't hope to disguise. Let her palm define the shape of him. Felt the life force pulsing urgently for release beneath her fingertips.

He shuddered. Groaned again. Attempted to hold her away.

Whimpering with need, she clawed at her dress, freeing

it from her shoulders and letting it glide in a silken whisper to her waist. She wore no bra underneath; no camisole. Nothing but a tan line dividing decency from forbidden pleasures.

His gaze seared her nakedness and she knew, from the sudden flood of color darkening his face, that she'd won. Dipping his head, he kissed her ear and whispered, in language erotically explicit, how he was going to love her and make her forget. And then, he proceeded to show her.

He cupped her bare breasts and took their aching peaks in his mouth, drawing so deeply at their core that she felt her soul slip away. He trailed his tongue in a slow, tormenting path down her cleavage to dally with her navel, then toured back, circuitously and at excruciating leisure, to her mouth.

Whatever secrets she had hidden there, he discovered with deft and expert thrusts and swirls. His tongue tasted of cognac and her perfume.

With one hand supporting her back, he took his other and slid it with delicious intent to the slit in the front of her skirt. Slow torture turned to raging gratification as his finger inched up her inner thigh and slipped inside the fine lace border edging the leg of her panties. If he hadn't known before that she was hot and sleek with hunger for him, he soon discovered that, too.

He was a devil and an angel, and she was so helplessly in thrall to his fondling that the best she could manage was to cling to him like a wilting vine as the spasms of completion he induced rolled over her.

When her knees threatened to buckle, he released her side zipper and with one sweep of his hand sent her dress and panties into a silken puddle on the floor, then lifted her into his arms and carried her to one of the couches. While she lay there with echoes of pleasure still rippling in the distant recesses of her body, he stripped off his own clothes and what he laid bare to her passion-glazed eyes was awesome to behold.

Of its own volition, her hand reached out, only to be halted by his while still inches from its destination. "Let me touch you," she pleaded. "Let me give pleasure to you."

His eyes caressed her face. "I'm not finished with you yet," he said, his voice overlaid with velvet.

"But I can't...not again, Sebastian...." Limp and depleted, she closed her eyes and felt tears pool along her lashes.

He parted her thighs, found her with the tip of his tongue and when she arched convulsively, brought his lips back to hers and whispered against her mouth, "Yes, you can, my lovely Lily. And when I'm deep inside you, you'll come again."

She was sure he was wrong. Would have found pleasure and satisfaction enough in accommodating him, in holding him close to her heart as his urgent thrusts took him closer to the edge of oblivion. Instead she caught the rhythm, climbed with him past the point of no return, then convulsed around him to milk the passion spilling from him and secrete it deep within herself.

The scented aftermath of their loving permeated the night, an elusive blend of skin and heat, of aftershave and perfume and fine French brandy, of man and woman and sex. His labored breathing punctuated the silence. His weight pressed her into the cool, smooth leather of the couch. His limbs, tangled with hers, held her his prisoner. And all the while, in her most intimate and secret place, he remained joined to her, a spent warrior at rest.

How long, if they'd had the choice, they'd have drifted together like that she never discovered, because another sound disturbed the night: that of the lower door from the stables opening and footsteps ascending the winding staircase, and Natalie's voice calling out, "Sebastian, you beast, are you here? I've been looking everywhere for you. We need to talk."

Lily's breath caught in a horrified gasp. Her eyes shot open, slewed across the room to the window where her dress lay like a puddle of ink on the pale oak floor. The diamanté heel of one of her shoes sparkled gleefully in the moonlight. Sebastian's shirt lay hooked on the corner of the coffee table, shining like a beacon to advertise his undressed presence.

Her limbs, which mere seconds before, had possessed all the strength and resilience of overcooked pasta, tensed. Completely unhinged, she swung her gaze back to Sebastian still stretched out on top of her, her eyes spelling out the words that surely must've been pounding through his mind, too. *What are we going to do?*

He gave an infinitesimal shake of his head and quietly laid his hand over her mouth before she could give voice to the question. And Natalie, having reached the landing, began making her way down the hall toward the living room.

CHAPTER SEVEN

"SEBASTIAN?" Her steps grew nearer and came to a stop so close to the couch that Lily's lungs seized up in anticipation of the scene about to unfold. Oh, the indignity of being caught in so compromising a situation! The shame!

Panic-stricken, she struggled to find an explanation—something...*anything!*—which would lessen the magnitude of the embarrassment consuming her. And the best she could come up with was, *Natalie, this isn't what it looks like.*

The utter absurdity of such a statement sent her into a paroxysm of silent hysterical giggles. Feeling the ripples chasing through her, Sebastian gave a faint, admonishing shake of his head, and buried her face against his shoulder.

Then Natalie's voice came again. "Hmm...wonder if he went to pick up Penny after her shift ended? Maybe he's already back at the party with her, and I've missed my chance *again*...."

Praise heaven and a benevolent God, her footsteps were fading toward the stairs! Shortly after, the lower door thudded closed.

Sebastian waited a full two minutes before moving: a small eternity of time that left Lily suspended somewhere between acute appreciation of the narrowness of their escape, and the fact that their naked bodies still lay entwined in the ultimate intimacy. But the magic of the moment, if, indeed, there'd ever been any, had left with Natalie, and if Lily had thought to presume otherwise, Sebastian soon disabused her of the idea.

The second he deemed it safe to do so, he rolled off the couch and disappeared down the hall. Shivering for all kinds of reasons, not the least being the sudden absence of his warm body on top of hers, Lily shot across the room and attempted to climb into both items of her discarded clothing at the same time.

Not a wise move, she quickly discovered, yanking viciously on her dress and hopping around on one foot as the other became hopelessly snarled in folds of fabric.

A table lamp clicked on. "No need to ruin a perfectly good outfit. Natalie went away convinced there was no one home. The odds of anyone else showing up unannounced are negligible," Sebastian observed, sauntering back into view decently covered in a navy terry-cloth bathrobe.

Feeling at a decided disadvantage with her panties hanging at half-mast around her knees, Lily grabbed the dress and used it to shield herself from his inspection—as if he hadn't already seen his fill! "How can you stand there and calmly behave as if what just happened wasn't a near disaster?"

"Are you referring to Natalie's untimely arrival, or the fact that you and I got rather carried away in the heat of the moment?"

"Both!" she cried, her nerves so brittle she felt ready to snap in half. "You're supposed to be dating another woman, yet you don't think twice about making love to me, and when we're almost caught in the act, you just lie there and wait to be discovered."

He shrugged and picked up the brandy decanter. "Sure you wouldn't like a shot of this to settle you down? No...? Okay...." He poured himself a refill and cupped his hands around the delicate balloon glass in much the same way he'd held her face not half an hour before. "First, to set the record straight, *you* were the instigator of our sexual encounter, not I."

The truth of that allegation sent a blush sweeping through her like wildfire. "Well, you didn't exactly rebuff me."

"No, Lily," he said evenly. "I suspect not many men would have turned down such a charmingly insistent proposition. We are, after all, mere mortals, just like women. And you are a very persuasive and accomplished seductress when you put your mind to it."

"Are you so fixated on sex that you don't see the bigger picture here? *What if Natalie had found us?*"

Smothering a sigh, he paced the width of the room. "It's because I *do* see the bigger picture that I can't worry about something that didn't happen. Tonight I betrayed the trust of a man who's been father, friend and mentor to me for longer than I care to remember and who never, except for this one thing, asked for any kind of return on his investment."

"I gather you're referring to the fact that you told me about my mother?" she said, scrambling into her dress while his back was turned. "Well, if you're worried I'm going to run to Hugo with the news—"

He spun around, his glance so loaded with rage, it was a miracle he didn't self-destruct. "I don't give a damn what you do! It's what *I've* done that'll keep me awake all night, and if you think I can just sweep my actions under the carpet and forget them, you know even less about the kind of man I am than I thought. So spare me your heroics, please! Hugo will learn his secret's out, but he'll hear it from me, not you, first thing tomorrow. I might have acted unethically, but I've not yet sunk to the level of cowardice.''

"And that's the only regret you have?"

"Should there be another?"

His contemptuous indifference to what the two of them had so recently shared should have burned her. Instead it chilled her to the bone. "Some might say the fact that we risked an unplanned pregnancy tonight might be cause for concern.''

He drew his hand down his face as if, by doing so, he could erase the entire evening. "Thank you for reminding me that, on top of everything else, I didn't use a condom. I suppose it's too much to hope you're on the pill?''

"I'm not on the pill. Casual sex isn't a recreational pastime for me and, unlike you, I'm not involved in a serious relationship with anyone." She stepped into her shoes and tried to finger-comb into place all the loose ends which had fallen out of her elegant hairdo. "Which brings up another point—how would Penny feel if she were to find out you and I had…?''

"Had sex?" He smiled bitterly. "Well, that's one secret I *am* prepared to keep, nor do I imagine you're too anxious to broadcast your indiscretion.''

"It was your indiscretion, too," she reminded him, dismayed all over again by how much his easy dismissal of their lovemaking hurt. "I might have started it, but you didn't seem to have too much trouble joining in and finishing off.''

He rounded on her, the anger formerly directed at himself turned now on her. "You want me to tell you I'm swimming in guilt about that, too? Fine, you've got it! I'm the world's biggest jerk. I should be strung up by my thumbs—unless there's some other section of my anatomy you'd prefer to see surgically removed. But I'm not a magician. I can't turn back the clock. What's done is done and we're both going to have to live with it.''

"Was there nothing memorable about it, Sebastian?" she asked, tears stinging her eyes and choking her voice. "Were you just going through the motions? Would it have been just as easy to turn me down?"

"If it had been, I'd have done that," he told her, a hint of tenderness warming his tone. "But I can't give you what you really want, Lily, and that's what makes sex between us wrong."

"What is it you think I want?"

"Love," he said simply. "It's one reason, maybe even the chief reason, you came to Stentonbridge in the first place. The loss of your immediate family has left you vulnerable and that by itself gives you enormous appeal." He took a step closer and brushed his knuckles down her cheek. "It would be very easy to ignore my conscience and embark on a summer affair with you. I'd be lying if I didn't admit the attraction's there, *and* the opportunity to give in to it. But we aren't *in love,* Lily. We don't even like each other very much, most of the time. And I've seen too many lives turned into a living hell because people mistook good sex for something deeper and more enduring. I'm not about to make the same mistake myself, especially not with Hugo Preston's daughter. I owe him better than that."

Everything he said made perfect sense. Trying to elevate lust to love was preposterous. Laughable. So why was she having such a hard time holding back the tears? Why did she feel as if she'd just found something precious, only to have it snatched away from her grasp before she could gain firm hold of it?

"You're absolutely right, of course. A summer fling

doesn't do it for me. I do want more. I want commitment from a man. Permanence.''

"And I'm not able to offer you either, not now and perhaps not ever."

"Of course not, nor do I expect you to." Since looking him in the eye was out of the question, she turned to stare out of the window and called up every last iota of pride to get her through what had to be said. "I think the least damage all around would be for us to forget everything that's transpired between us in this room tonight. Don't burden Hugo with your confessions, Sebastian, and let's not burden each other with useless regrets."

"I have to tell him."

"No." She shook her head, and the motion set the tears in her eyes to shimmering and blinding her vision. "Don't risk your relationship with him because of what you've told me. It's enough that I finally know the truth."

"I can't promise I'll abide by that, Lily."

"Well, you'd damn well better," she cried, wheeling toward the stairs. "If you care about him as much as you say you do, you won't ease your conscience at his expense. You'll learn to live with what you know, just as I have to."

She got no farther than the landing before he caught up with her. "Where do you think you're going?"

"Anywhere, as long as it's away from you!"

"I'm afraid not," he said. "By now, we'll surely have been missed at the party. If you're serious about not wanting to arouse everyone's suspicions, we're going to reappear, together, and act as if nothing untoward has taken place. If anyone asks, we went for a stroll by the river."

She couldn't do it. As far as he was concerned, her acting repertoire had exhausted itself. She couldn't pretend she was fine when her heart felt as if he'd stamped the imprint of his heel on it. "You're hardly dressed for the part," she said, shrugging off his hand, "and I'm perfectly capable of making up my own lies to explain my absence, without any help from you."

"You're a mess," he said brutally. "You couldn't fool an infant, let alone anyone as perceptive as Hugo." He steered her past the stairwell and shoved her into a powder room near the other end of the hall. "Splash some cold water on your face and fix your hair while I get ready. It won't take me more than a couple of minutes."

She looked in the mirror over the sink. A stranger stared back, wild-eyed and disheveled. The chain of her pendant was snagged in a section of hair trailing down her neck. She was wearing only one earring. Her lipstick was smeared, her mascara had run. He was right: she was a walking advertisement of sated passion and grief.

Somehow she managed to repair the worst of the damage to her face, though anyone looking closely at her reddened eyes would surely know she'd been crying. Restoring her elegant, upswept hairdo was another matter, and in the end she pulled out all the pins and let it fall loose to her shoulders.

Sebastian was waiting for her when she came out and, certainly, no one would have guessed he'd recently been rolling around naked. He looked as coolly unperturbed as if he'd spent the entire evening reading law books in Hugo's library. His bow tie lay precisely where it should against his shirt which shone crisp and fresh as new snow. His jacket clung with immaculate precision to his shoulders.

"Ready?" he asked.

"No. I'm missing an earring." She scanned the floor by the window. "I must have lost it here, but I don't see it."

"I'll look for it later. With your hair down like that, no one's going to notice." He surveyed her critically. "I won't say you look as good as new, but you'll fool the people who matter. Let's go."

He preceded her down the stairs and led her out and around the back of the stables to another path, which followed the course of the river. "Gives more credibility to our story, should anyone ask," he said, tucking her hand into the crook of his elbow. "Smile, for Pete's sake. You look as if you lost your best friend, instead of just an earring."

"I did," she said stonily. "Thanks to you, I just found out my mother wasn't who she pretended to be."

"I tried to spare you, but you're the one who insisted on knowing."

"Right now, I'm not in the mood for any *I told you so's*, Sebastian."

"No," he said thoughtfully. "I don't suppose I would be, either, in your place. Does it help at all to know I didn't gain an ounce of pleasure or satisfaction from enlightening you and that I wish I could have been the bearer of better news?"

"Not much. It doesn't change anything."

They rounded a bank of rhododendrons and found themselves back on the lower lawn. The party had clearly wound down, leaving only a handful of guests remaining at the small tables on the terrace. "Uh-oh," Sebastian muttered, as all eyes turned their way. "I hoped we'd be able to merge with the crowd. Instead we're making an entrance. Just keep your smile pinned in place and leave the talking to me."

She did and wished she could admire his accounting of their absence, presenting the facts as logically and persuasively as if he were trying to convince a courtroom judge. Instead she hated him for his ability to shift gears so effortlessly. Shakespeare, she decided bitterly, had been right when he'd written, *Let's kill all the lawyers!*

After that night, Sebastian didn't see her again for nearly two weeks. He wished he could as easily get her out of his mind but his conscience wouldn't allow it. As if it wasn't bad enough that he'd spilled secrets that weren't his to share, he'd compounded matters by making love with her.

No use trying to trivialize the experience by labeling it as nothing but sex, because it had amounted to more than that. They *had* made love and in such spectacular fashion that whatever interest he'd once had in Penny Stanford had withered overnight.

Even worse, he'd betrayed Hugo a second time by taking advantage of his daughter when she was most vulnerable and even if Hugo could forgive him for that, he couldn't forgive himself.

What was it about her that made her so hard to forget? Her fragility? Her vulnerability when she learned the truth about her mother? Or was it just that he felt sorry for her?

Hell, no! It wasn't pity stirring to life down below his belt whenever he recalled their night of love, and it wasn't charity!

Then, on top of everything else, there was the latest report from the investigator. The information it contained should have vindicated his suspicions about her. Instead it sat in his gut like lead and he wished he'd never embarked on the inquiry in the first place. *Suspicion of fraud and conspiracy* were ugly words in any context. He didn't want to believe they applied to her—and if *that* didn't go to show what bad shape he was in, maybe it was time he retired from the law and went to work collecting other people's garbage!

On the Thursday of the week following the party, his mother phoned him at the office. "Just wanted to remind you we're going up to the cottage tomorrow afternoon, and spending the weekend there, Sebastian. You'll come with us, of course?"

To stare Lily straight in the eye and behave as if the most they'd ever shared was a cool handshake? To pretend he didn't know how she'd trembled beneath him and begged him with her eyes and her hands and her little urgent cries, to come to her as she hovered on the brink of orgasm? To know he could look as she paraded around in her skinny little bathing suit, but he couldn't touch? And worst of all, to act as if he didn't know she was under police investigation in Vancouver?

"I don't think so," he said. "I'm bogged down with work right now."

"But that leak in the flashing around the chimney needs to be fixed before it damages the bedroom ceiling, and I can't have Hugo climbing ladders to the roof at his age! And we've done so much entertaining since Lily arrived that I thought a quiet weekend with just the family would make for a nice change." His mother's voice sharpened with disappointment. "Honestly, Sebastian, I can't believe you forgot, though I suppose I shouldn't be too surprised since you haven't shown your face at the house in days."

"If you must know, I thought Lily would be heading home any day now and you'd changed your mind. Didn't she plan to stay here only about three weeks?"

"Yes. But her father's convinced her to stay until the Labor Day weekend since there's no pressing need for her to fly home any sooner."

Oh, terrific! One more complication he didn't need!

"So, what do you say, Sebastian? Will you join us? You can bring your work with you, if you like. You won't be the only one. Natalie's going to have to study part of the time, too, with her finals coming up soon. But it would mean a lot to Hugo to have you there. You know how much he enjoys a man's company, especially yours, and he's noticed that you seem to be avoiding coming to the house."

Because I'm ashamed to see him—or Lily!

But in the end, and against his better judgment, he agreed to his mother's request. He told himself it was because he had to face Hugo sooner or later but there was more to it than that, and he knew it. His attraction to Lily Talbot was out of control. For all that he wished it were otherwise, when the opportunity presented itself, he couldn't stay away from her.

Still, when he arrived at the lake the next evening, he tried to keep his distance and, apparently, succeeded too well. Natalie cornered him in the kitchen where she'd coerced him into helping her clean up after dinner, and wasted no time getting straight to the point. "You've told her, haven't you?"

"Told who what?"

"You've spilled the beans to Lily about her mother."

He made a big production of stowing stuff into the refrigerator. "What makes you think that?"

"Oh, I don't know!" she drawled sarcastically. "Perhaps because neither one of you can stand looking the other in the eye. Or perhaps it's got more to do with the fact that every time she opens her mouth to speak, you act as if she's not even in the room, but then, when you think no one's noticing, you watch her like a hawk hovering over its next meal. You *did* tell her, didn't you?"

He heaved a weary sigh and leaned against the refrigerator door. "If you must know, yes, I did. And I wish I hadn't."

"I don't," she said. "I think she deserved to be told. In fact, I came looking for you the night of Dad's birthday party, to try to convince you to tell her, but you'd disappeared."

And you'll never know how close you came to finding me, Nat! "Yes. Revealing family secrets with an audience of a hundred didn't seem such a hot idea, so we...went off by ourselves."

"How did she take the news?"

He rolled his eyes. For someone bent on a career in social work, Natalie could be astonishingly obtuse when it came to understanding people. "How do you think!"

"Not well. I can see in her eyes that she's pretty torn up about it. Does Dad know?"

"That I've told her? No."

"Well, if you don't want him to guess for himself, you'd better get cracking on some sort of damage control. I've thought ever since the party that she's been quieter than usual, but it wasn't until you showed up tonight that I figured out why. Heck, Sebastian, I thought she was going to faint when she saw you!"

It wasn't often that he followed Natalie's nineteen-year-old advice but, for once, she had a point worth taking. He strolled out to the porch and found Lily, with Katie at her feet, chatting idly with Hugo and his mother. Slapping the flat of his hand to his waist, he said casually, "I need to walk off that meal. Come with me, Lily, and I'll show you the neighborhood."

He saw the stubborn cast to her chin and knew she was about to refuse him. Hauling her off the wicker love seat, he marched her down the steps before she could voice her protest aloud and strong-armed her down the path to the lakefront. "Don't bother telling me you'd rather keep company with a pit viper," he informed her, when they were out of sight and earshot. "I've already received that message loud and clear. But I need to talk to you. Privately."

"I hope it's urgent," she snapped, massaging her wrist. "I don't appreciate being man-handled like this. And if you've dug up more dirt on my mother, you can keep it. I'm not bartering my self-respect a second time to hear things better left unsaid."

He caught her elbow and pulled her around to face him. "Lily, please!"

"Don't touch me!" Angrily she shrugged him off.

He raised both hands in surrender. "Okay. I won't touch you. But will you at least hear me out?"

"Do I have any choice?"

She was putting up a good front, but he could see the effort it cost her. Her eyes were glazed with tears, her voice shook. "Look," he said gently, "I can see you've gone through hell, this last couple of weeks, but if it makes you feel any better, it's been no walk in the park for me, either."

"Why? Because you broke your promise to Hugo?"

He nodded. "I should have listened to him. Respected his judgment, his wisdom. He recognized from the first that your knowing about Genevieve's mistakes would cause nothing but unnecessary trouble and hurt."

"I've come to terms with her mistakes," Lily said flatly. "She wasn't perfect, but who is? Not Hugo and certainly not you or I. Yes, I was shocked to hear what had happened, but I can live with it because there's another truth that counts for more than things that happened before I was born. Whatever her faults, Genevieve was a good mother. *Both* my parents were the best—and I'm not talking about Hugo when I say that.''

"Then why are you still so unhappy? I found your earring, if that's what's bothering you. I was planning to get it back to you but hadn't figured out how to do so discreetly. I didn't think you'd appreciate my presenting it to you in front of everyone else, and saying I'd found it between the cushions of my couch.''

She stared at him. "You have the nerve to suggest a piece of jewelry is the reason I'm upset?''

He couldn't remember the last time he'd blushed but he knew for a fact it was well before his tenth birthday. As if to make up for the time elapsed since then, an embarrassing heat spread over his face. "Of course not. It's because we...were together.''

"Good heavens, Sebastian, don't try to sugarcoat the facts now!'' she said scornfully. "We *screwed!* Had a one-night stand! Isn't that how you men phrase it when you're intimate with a woman you don't care about and never want to see again, once the romp between the sheets—or, in this case, the sliding around on your leather couch—is over?''

"Stop it, Lily! I won't listen to that kind of talk.''

"Why? Am I making you uncomfortable? Speaking the truth too plainly?''

"It's not the truth, and you know it.''

"No?'' A lone tear, bright as a diamond, trembled on her lower lashes. "Well, here's something that is. I feel cheap and dirty because of the way I behaved with you. You might not have been my first lover, but you are the first man who made me feel like a whore!''

"Don't talk like that!'' Overcoming her efforts to evade him, he grabbed hold of her again. "And unless you want to hurt yourself, stop fighting me. Because I'm not letting go."

"Yes, you are," she cried, aiming a kick at his shin and, when she missed, bursting into tears of frustration.

As it had more than once before, her mouth reminded him of a rose carelessly crushed underfoot. Her eyes wore the look of bruised pansies. When he pulled her into the shelter of his arms, the sobs shaking her body made her feel as frail as the thin glazing of ice that covered the lake in early winter and crumbled at a touch.

"You want to know something?" he muttered, rocking her against him and burying his face in her hair. "I wish I *had* been your first lover. I wish I'd been the one to teach you what passion's all about. And I wish we could have met under different circumstances. Perhaps if we had…"

Even though he left the sentence unfinished, she guessed the direction his thoughts had been taking. "We might have fallen in love?" She drew in a tortured breath. "I don't think so, Sebastian. Love doesn't come calling only when it's convenient. It's not that calculating, or that easily controlled."

Nor was desire! Holding her close again revived the same pulsing ache that had gotten him into so much trouble two weeks before. Rational thought dissolved into hot, urgent need. She was warm to his touch, her skin soft. So smooth and satin soft he wanted to stroke her all over. And taste her—the delicate flower fragrance of her mouth, the sweet secret honey of her femininity.

She tilted her face up to his. The fading light touched her tear tracks with gold, sparkled on her wet lashes, kissed the curve of her mouth with a familiarity he resented. "Please let me go, Sebastian," she whispered. "I can't bear your being kind to me like this."

"But it isn't kindness." His voice became trapped in a throat grown thick with an emotion that didn't bear close analysis, something that went beyond mere passion. "God help me, I want you, Lily. More than ever. And I think you want me, too."

She looked away and refused to answer.

He gave her a little shake, slight enough, to be sure, but it didn't take much for the undulation of her body against his to increase his hunger to fever pitch. "Don't you?" he persisted urgently.

"Stop cross-examining me," she retorted. "You're not in the courtroom now, and I'm not on trial."

"Answer the question," he begged, against her mouth. "And if I'm wrong, I'll let you go."

"Oh, I want you," she said hopelessly. "And I despise myself for it."

Above them on the rise of land where the cottage stood, a sudden flood of light spilled into the dusk. Anyone standing at the windows would easily spot them, might even think to join them for the neighborhood tour he'd so flippantly come up with as an excuse to get her alone. Never mind that his reason for doing so had changed. What mattered now was that they not be deflected from a course as inevitable as the pattern of early stars pricking the sky.

"There's a dinghy in the boathouse," he said, turning back to the foot of the path that had brought them to the waterfront. "Come out on the lake with me. We'll be alone there, with no chance of anyone walking in on us."

She hesitated. Pulled away from him until the tips of their fingers barely touched, yet he felt her indecision as clearly as if he were grasping a live electric wire.

"Please," he said, increasing his hold and inching her back toward him. "Come with me, Lily."

CHAPTER EIGHT

THE lake was limpid as smoked glass. Except for the muted slap of the oars and the cry of a distant loon, not a sound broke the silence of the night. Rowing swiftly, he angled the boat to the far side of an island lying about a mile offshore.

"We used to come here as kids," he said, after they'd waded onto the sliver of beach and he'd tied up the dinghy to a nearby tree.

"And as adults?"

A simple enough question on the surface, but he heard another in her voice and said, "I've never brought a woman here until tonight, Lily, if that's what you're asking. You're the first."

He tried to catch her hand and draw her to him, but she slipped away and walked parallel to the water, head bent and footsteps whispering in the soft, white sand. She wore shorts and a cotton top. Her skin, tanned honey-gold by day, took on a richer tone in the gloom against the pale color of her clothes. Her hair, caught back in combs, spilled down her back dark as midnight silk.

Although he'd have preferred to have her close in his arms, viewing her from a distance gave him a better appreciation of her slender elegance. How had he missed it, when they'd first met? Wherever had he come up with the idea that she was unremarkable? Her kind of understated good looks put more flamboyant beauty to shame.

When she'd gone about twenty yards, she stopped and

turned to face him. Her voice carried clearly in the night. "I don't suppose I'll be the last, though," she said.

He lifted his shoulders in a shrug. "I don't know. But I do know every time I tell myself that becoming involved with you is a bad idea, another part of me doesn't want to accept it."

"I can imagine which part!"

"I'm talking about a connection that goes beyond physical attraction."

"But you can't put a name to it. Or won't." There was no missing the barbed edge in her words.

"You want me to call it love, but we both know it's too soon for that." He stifled a sigh. "We've known each other less than two months. Can't we agree to table definitions until the end of the summer, and just let things evolve at their own pace? See how things work out between us?"

"Sneak around having sex, you mean, but lead the family to believe we're just good friends?"

"Would it be so bad if friendship's the best we could manage?"

"But we won't manage that, and we both know it." The moon slid out from behind the low rise of hills to the east. Limned in its light, she looked achingly lonely and vulnerable. "When an affair goes sour, Sebastian, it never ends in friendship. It ends in pain and bitterness and regret."

He couldn't look that far down the line. There were too many unknowns. "All I really know at this minute is that I want to hold you." He opened his arms. "Come here, sweetheart, please."

She scuffed her bare toes in the sand and dragged her feet, an outward show of resistance to combat the desire she couldn't deny so exactly mirroring his own ambiva-

lence that he almost smiled. But the way she was looking
at him, the sultry curve of her mouth, the way she ran her
tongue over her upper lip and let her hand trail sugges-
tively all the way from her throat to her breast and down
the length of her thigh, were no laughing matter. They
spoke of passion about to be unleashed, of a magnetic
pull that had her suddenly giving in to its force and running toward him.

He met her halfway and they collapsed together on the
cool sand. Her mouth softened beneath his. Opened.
Welcomed. Her fingers inched inside his shirt, traced
lightly over his ribs, slid to his navel.

The heat in his belly raged, left him throbbing. He
wanted to savor the moment, enjoy the feast she presented. Dwell in close detail on every satin inch of her.
But a dozen demons drove him, savaging his control. He
had to have her...now...!

Dimly he heard cotton and denim shrieking softly as
they were flung aside; the protesting gasp of silky under-
things too roughly handled. He felt her, hot and moist
against his cupped hand, heard her inarticulate little cry
when he touched her sensitized flesh.

She deserved to be loved with leisurely expertise. With
finesse and sophistication, and respect. But he'd left it too
late, tormented himself for too long. There was room for
nothing in his universe but the sheer heaven of finding
himself inside her and then, mere seconds later, losing
himself inside her, utterly and completely.

Eventually he lifted his head and looked down at her.
Her mouth was swollen from his kisses, her eyes luminous
in the moonlight. "I should probably apologize for that,"
he said, when his breathing allowed him to speak,
"but regret isn't the emotion uppermost in my mind
right now."

The slow, sweet radiance of her smile and the way she stroked the hair off his forehead moved him unbearably. Flirtation, teasing, sexual gratification pure and simple— these things he could deal with in a woman. But tenderness, Lily Talbot style, left him wide-open to a baffling array of emotions.

Too bad that regret sat so close to the top of the list!

Averting his gaze, Sebastian wished for the umpteenth time that he'd accepted her at face value and never started the investigative process. Just knowing that all the time they were making love, his West Coast spy was compiling an ever-incriminating dossier that laid bare every particle of her life for his inspection, made him ill.

Pursue this and send more details, he'd instructed his man, but the guy had run up against a brick wall. Police weren't forthcoming about ongoing investigations, and the odds were he'd learn nothing new until charges were laid.

"What are you thinking about?" Lily asked him softly.

Squirming inwardly at the uncomfortable shot of guilt flushing through him, he said, "That we should go swimming."

She gave a captivating gurgle of laughter. *"Here?"*

"Why not?" He circled her breast with one finger. "I seem to recall you like swimming after dark."

She laughed, a breathless, abbreviated gasp that told him how much she liked the way he was touching her, too. "I'd forgotten about that night in the pool."

"I hadn't," he said. "That was the first time I kissed you."

"You lied to me, as well. About wearing a swimsuit."

He was lying to her now, about something a whole hell of a lot more serious than being stark naked, and the knowledge was eating holes in him.

Mistaking his silence for confusion, she reminded him, "You said you were skinny-dipping."

"Well, this time I will be and so, my dear, will you."

He sprang to his feet and pulled her up after him. The sight of her, all moon-washed curves and shadows, reminded him again why he'd really brought her to this isolated spot. For crying out loud, he was worse than a randy eighteen-year-old in the back seat of his father's car with a high school cheerleader!

"Last one in's a chicken!" he taunted, sprinting to the water's edge and taking a flat, racing dive into the lake guaranteed to shock the most active libido into submission.

Her laughter chased him and when he surfaced a hundred yards from shore, he found her bobbing beside him, her hair streaming out behind her, her eyes blacker than the night except for the pinpoints of stars reflected in her pupils.

She closed her eyes, and folding her hands behind her head, floated on her back. Her nipples showed just above the surface, tiny islands of temptation just beyond his reach. She sighed blissfully. "The water's so warm, it's like a bath in here!"

"Yeah," he said ruefully, gaining a foothold on the rise of a sand bank in the shallow depths. "Where's a cold shower when a guy needs one? I'm aching for you again already, Lily."

The laughter on her face faded. She flipped herself upright and floated closer, sculling gently with her hands. Her legs tangled briefly with his, then drifted away again. Her shoulders looked as if they'd been dipped in silver.

"Why can't I seem to get enough of you, Sebastian?" she asked seriously, fixing her gaze on his mouth. "Why do I risk getting hurt by letting myself fall under your spell time and again?''

Absently he twirled a lock of her hair around his finger, plagued by another question he wished he dared ask. *How can you be so open and honest on the one hand and, on the other, capable of the kind of duplicity that my investigator's report suggests?*

She tipped her head to one side and touched her hand to his jaw. "Sebastian? What's troubling you suddenly?"

"What makes you think anything is?"

He attempted to laugh off her concern, but she held his gaze. "I can see it in your face."

He wished he could tell her. Wished he could just come right out and say, *Look, I know you're in some sort of trouble back home, that you could be facing legal action. Come clean with me, and I'll help you. No one else in the family needs to know. I'm a lawyer, professionally and personally committed to protecting client confidentiality. But as long as you keep this secret, there's a barrier between us that's crippling any chance we might have of developing a lasting relationship.*

The trouble was, for him to admit he'd gone behind her back in the first place would deal a death blow to what they shared. She'd never forgive him and he could hardly expect she would.

"Rule number one—don't go looking for problems where they don't exist, Lily," he said, looping his arm around her neck. "Just savor the moment."

She bit her lip and lowered her eyes, and he knew she was hurt by his evasion.

To make up for it, he tugged her close enough to leave no doubt as to how he proposed to make that moment memorable. "You're beautiful by moonlight, did you know that?"

Her eyes flew up to meet his. She looked almost embarrassed. "You've never said anything like that to me before."

"Then I've been very remiss. I should have told you a long time ago."

"Is that another of your rules—to flatter a woman into submission? Because if it is, you ought to know by now that you don't have to go to such lengths. I know I'm not beautiful. I'm merely...pleasant looking." She parted her thighs and trapped him between their soft inner contours. "And very...very...willing..."

He shaped her with his hands, stunned once again by her perfect symmetry: the narrow span of her waist and slender flare of her hips, the sweet, full curve of her buttocks. "Oh, you're a lot more than that," he murmured, slipping inside her and exhaling sharply as she closed around him sleek as a glove. "You're...irresistible."

Their coming together this time was slow and exquisite, the thrust and retreat in sync with the flow of the water around them. If he could, he'd have loved her like that all night, riding the gentle waves and warding off the climax lurking in the darkness like some predatory beast waiting to destroy him.

But she decided otherwise, wrapping her long, golden legs around his waist, tormenting him with her mouth, whispering in his ear how he pleased her, how she loved the power and drive of him. Begging him in a voice close to a sob to touch her "...right there...like that...oh... yes!"

And he was lost. Shattered. He heard himself cry out her name, his voice a razor-edge of anguish bordered with ecstasy. His seed surged free, and took his soul with it. Depleted him so exhaustively that it was all he could do to remain afloat. Indeed wouldn't have, if it hadn't been that the water was no more than five feet deep and he could anchor his feet to the sandy bottom.

She clung to him, her breath winnowing in warm, damp gusts against his neck. "Oh, Sebastian!" she murmured, drenching his name in the aftermath of passion. "*I love*...how you make me feel!"

She had been on the verge of saying something else. He knew by the subtle stiffening of her body, the way she suddenly reined in the impulsive flow of her words. And he couldn't begin to decipher his reaction; didn't have the first idea how to reconcile the chagrin that rolled over him because she hadn't said it, with the welling relief that she hadn't forced an issue he wasn't ready to deal with.

"Know what?" he said, grazing her mouth with his reply. "We'd better get back before someone at the cottage realizes the boat's gone and they send out a search party to look for us."

She didn't have to tell him it wasn't the response she'd been hoping for. The way she dropped her arms and drifted away from him, then turned and swam quickly ashore, spoke volumes of disappointment.

Following, he caught up with her as she ran up the beach to where they'd left their clothes. "Lily," he began, searching for a way to soften his rejection without compromising his sense of decency any more than he already had.

She turned to him, a too-bright smile fixed in place. "You should have thought to bring towels. How are we going to explain the fact that our hair's soaking and our clothing damp?"

If only that was all he had to worry about! "With any luck, everyone will be in bed by the time we get back. If not, I'll distract them while you sneak in by the back door."

*   *   *

The cottage was old, built some time in the late nineteenth century. Though constructed to withstand the vicious winters, its floorboards creaked and its interior walls were thin. Even if his room hadn't been next to hers, she'd probably have been able to hear his every move.

With her window wide-open against the stifling heat of the Ontario summer, though, she knew to the second when he climbed into bed. By turning her head just a fraction, she could see where the glow from his reading lamp illuminated the near branches of the pine tree in the garden.

A moth batted against the screen at her window, then fluttered off in search of the source of light. *Just like me, poor fool,* she thought miserably. *Not happy until it scorches to death on its own folly.*

Next door, Sebastian extinguished the light. The mattress squeaked faintly as he turned over. Would he fall asleep easily, the lovemaking they'd shared already consigned to the past? Or, like her, lie awake in the dark and brood over where their relationship was headed?

She closed her eyes and relived that hour on the island. The first frenzied coming together over too soon, but still magnificent enough to leave her yearning for more. And then the next time…the velvet night, the water plush against her skin…

She felt again his body, sleek, slick, joining with hers and carrying her on a current of passion growing ever more urgent. Sweeping her toward rapids tantalizingly out of reach until, suddenly, with a rush that took her breath away, he hurled her over the edge.

Goose bumps pebbled her skin. Squirming, she pulled the sheet over her. It had been perfect. *Perfect!* Until, caught up in the emotion of the moment, the words hammering in her brain had burst forth.

Oh, she'd caught herself in time, turned *I love you!*—

an admission he didn't want to hear—into an innocuous *I love how you make me feel,* but he'd guessed how close she'd come to slipping up and breaking the rules he'd laid down. Any fool would have known, when her whole heart had revealed itself in the timbre of her voice. And Sebastian was no fool.

That second time they'd made love had been different, though. In the warm water of the lake, they'd merged softly—which was an odd word to use, considering he was all steel and unyielding strength. But she'd sensed a rare gentleness in him, a protectiveness almost. Inured as she'd become to his more abrasive nature, this other side of him had taken her by surprise and stolen past the defenses she'd thought she held so securely in place.

The pity of it was, she hadn't been content with small gifts. Like a child let loose in a candy store, she'd been greedy for more. When he'd hustled her into the boat and, instead of using the oars, had fired up the small outboard motor and propelled them back to the mainland with what struck her as taciturn haste, she'd said plaintively, ''Now that you've had your way with me, you seem in an almighty rush to get rid of me. A mistress—and a mistress on your terms—is all I seem to be.''

He'd lifted his head and subjected her to a stare so full of frustration that she could have cut out her tongue. ''I know that in all the best movies, this is the moment where the hero's supposed to announce that his intentions are honorable,'' he'd finally said, ''but I think we've already established we're a long way from anything remotely approaching that. If you're looking for some sort of commitment, you're knocking on the wrong door. The sex between us couldn't be better, but I thought we agreed that's as far as it goes right now.''

The worst of it was, he was absolutely right. They were

both long past the age where they allowed physical attraction to get in the way of common sense. But logic didn't carry much weight when feminine intuition was calling a different tune, and every instinct she possessed was sounding a clarion call that Sebastian Caine was the man she was destined to love.

Apparently she wasn't the only one nurturing such hopes. Just before noon on the Saturday, Penny Stanford showed up at the cottage. "Found your message waiting when I came off shift last night, Sebastian," she chirped, standing on her cute little tippytoes to kiss him in a way that left no doubt in anyone's mind that she considered herself at the head of the line for his attention, "and thought I'd invite myself up here for the day since I've seen next to nothing of you for the last few weeks."

"You're always welcome, Penny, you know that," Cynthia said.

"Thank you." Her smile flitted warmly over Hugo and Cynthia, then chilled noticeably as it skimmed over Natalie and then finally came to rest on Lily. "One more in such a crowd hardly makes any difference, does it? And I did pick up treats—those dear little shrimp pies from the deli that we love so much, Sebastian. And our favorite wine."

She batted her eyelashes in blatant promise of other treats intended just for him. "I was hoping we could slip away for a while, just the two of us, and catch up the news. Maybe go over to that island you once mentioned. I could use a little relaxation and if you don't mind my saying so, you look a bit peaked, too. Have you been getting enough rest?"

It was all Lily could do not to shriek out, *No, he hasn't! He was up half the night making love to me on that island you're so anxious to see, and if he takes you there as well, I'll rip his throat out!*

As if she sensed trouble brewing, Natalie poked Lily in the ribs and muttered, "Grab a towel and let's get out of here before I hurl!"

She waited until they'd cooled off in the lake and were stretched out on the sunbaked boards of the boat jetty before asking, "From the look on your face back there at the cottage, Lily, I'd say I'm not the only one who can't stand to be in the same room with Penny Stanford for more than five minutes."

"Oh, dear!" Lily looked up from folding her towel into a makeshift pillow. "Was it that obvious?"

"You practically turned green around the gills." Natalie giggled. "Not that I blame you! Imagine waking up after an operation and finding her face hanging over you! No wonder so many people get nauseated after an anesthetic. As for the little TLC act she put on for Sebastian's benefit...!"

Trying to be scrupulously fair, Lily said, "Perhaps she genuinely cares about him."

"And we don't?" Natalie shot her a scornful glance. "Anyway, let's forget about her and talk about something more interesting. I got some news yesterday, just before I left the college, and I'm so excited I can hardly stand myself. Once I've written my finals, I've been invited to go to India with eight other students to work under the supervision of a team of social workers and medical personnel in Bombay. If I accept—"

"What do you mean, *if?*" Lily exclaimed. "Natalie, it's a wonderful opportunity and a great compliment! Of course you'll accept!"

"I was hoping you'd say that, because I might need some help convincing Mom and Dad. In their eyes, I'm still the baby, barely able to cross the road without supervision. But with you on my side, I think I can talk them into letting me go. I have to give my answer on Tuesday, so maybe we can present the idea this afternoon, while dear old Penny is chasing Sebastian all over Snake Island.''

"*Snake* Island?"

"That's not what it's really called. In fact, I don't know if it even has an official name, but we've always called it that because we used to find so many snakes there when we were kids." She gave another infectious giggle. "Maybe one'll bite her!"

"If it does," Lily said sourly, "I guarantee its name will be Sebastian."

Selling Hugo and Cynthia on the idea of letting their daughter spend six weeks thousands of miles away in India was no easy task, but in the end, they agreed it was an opportunity not to be missed.

"Thanks, Lily," Natalie said later, as the two of them drove into the village to pick up a tub of ice cream to go with the strawberry tarts Cynthia had made for dessert. "I'm not sure I could have swung it if I hadn't had you there to back me up."

By the time they returned, the afternoon had dwindled away and taken the sunshine with it.

"Looks as if we might be in for a bit of weather," Hugo observed, scanning the far side of the lake where purple thunderheads were building above the horizon. "The dog's restless and the wind's picking up. I hope Sebastian thought to bring the dinghy into the boathouse."

"You mean he's here?" Lily looked up from setting

the table. "I thought he and his date were still on the island."

"No, they came back soon after you and Natalie left for the village. Penny headed back to town and Sebastian decided to follow her. It'll just be the four of us for dinner."

Wiping her hands on her apron, Cynthia came out of the kitchen. "I think we'd better put the pails out upstairs. I'm afraid we're in for a downpour and that flashing still hasn't been fixed around the chimney."

Sure enough, about nine o'clock, the storm picked up and blew across the lake with terrifying speed. One minute, the four of them were playing bridge by lamplight, and the next, Katie was cowering under the dining-room table as thunder rolled in the distance and the first blast of wind hit the house.

While Natalie helped her parents close all the windows and place pails and bowls to catch any water leaking through the ceiling, Lily ran down to the lake to make sure everything there was secured. But her flashlight showed her that although the sleek motor vessel used for waterskiing was secure inside the boathouse, the twelve-foot aluminum dinghy had been left tied to the jetty and was taking a relentless beating as the wind slammed it against the pilings.

Since she didn't have nearly the strength to haul it to safety onshore, her only choice was to lower herself into it and by hanging on to the rail edging the deck of the little dock, try to steer around to the wide double doors on the water side of the boathouse. A difficult task at the best of times, it was made that much worse by the driving rain that lashed her face and cut the already limited visibility to zero.

Before she'd even managed to cast off, she was soaked

to the skin. Freeing the dinghy from its mooring was a monumental undertaking, and only when she'd succeeded did she realize she'd merely compounded her difficulties. With nothing to anchor it, the boat tossed and bobbed like a cork, completely at the mercy of the weather.

Even sitting in the center of the seat, she'd have been hard-pressed to maintain her balance, but trying to stand, hold a flashlight in one hand and grasp the edge of the jetty with the other, was inviting disaster. Before she knew what was happening, a wave caught the side of the boat and flipped it over. In horrible slow motion, she saw the water coming up to meet her, then the dark shadow of the hull rising above her.

The painter attached to the bow snaked around her ankle. A vicious gust of wind sent the upturned boat lumbering forward and threatening to crush her between it and the pilings supporting the jetty. A wave buried her and she realized in stunned disbelief that she was in danger of drowning in ten feet of water, with land less than ten yards away. It shouldn't have been possible, but it was happening.

Well, damn it, she wouldn't allow it!

Choking and spluttering, she clung to the hull of the dinghy with one hand and with the other struggled to free her ankle from the rope. Was that what caused the boat to turn turtle again—her putting her weight too much on one side and the waves pushing too hard from the other? Or was she engaged in a losing battle from the first? Whatever the reason, it slowly heaved up like some prehistoric creature, turned slowly on its side and started filling with water.

As the painter around her ankle tightened, Lily tasted a fear like nothing she'd ever known before. A scream tore loose from her throat and, involuntarily, a name. *"Sebastian!"*

A light appeared, weaving erratically down the path from the cottage and, miraculously, he was there, racing along the jetty and flinging a lifeline to her. "Let go of the boat!" he shouted, aiming the lantern he carried so that he could see her. "Push yourself away from it and I'll pull you in."

"I can't," she gasped, sobbing the words between breaths that burned her lungs like fire. "I'm trapped in the mooring line."

"The hell you are!" In a flash, he'd dumped the lantern on the dock and was in the water beside her. The blade of a knife glimmered as he raised his hand. And then, blessedly, the awful tension around her ankle lessened and he had her by the scruff of the neck and was towing her ashore. She had never felt anything as welcome as the fine gravel scoring her knees and elbows as he heaved her above the waterline.

For the longest time, she lay in a heap, incapable of speech or movement. When she at last lifted her head, she found him kneeling beside her. "You know," he said, "you've really got to stop this business of swimming after dark. You're obviously not very good at it."

"I know," she said, and tried to smile. Instead she burst into tears. "I thought I was going to die," she wailed, burying her face against his sodden shirt. "I thought the boat would sink and take me with it, and I'd never see any of you again."

"Fat chance! For a start, it's designed not to sink. And you're not getting rid of us that easily," he said roughly.

But his hand was gentle on her hair, his arm tight and comforting around her shoulders. And when she lifted her face to his, his mouth closing over hers was warm and tender.

"You're turning into one big headache for me, you know that?" he murmured, when they came up for air. "What the devil am I going to do with you?"

CHAPTER NINE

THE storm blew itself out before midnight. The next morning, Sebastian repaired the roof, Hugo mopped up the damage inside the cottage and Natalie and Lily cleaned up outside while Cynthia prepared lunch on the screened porch.

Sebastian was the last to join them. He took his place at the foot of the table, with Natalie on his right and Lily on his left. Before he'd even helped himself to the cold chicken salad, Natalie began quizzing him. "What made Penny leave early? We practically have to evict her, as a rule."

"Natalie!" Cynthia's eyebrows rose in reproof.

"Oh, Mom, it's true and you know it! You said yourself you were surprised she only stayed a couple of hours."

"Perhaps," Sebastian said mildly, amusement flickering at the corners of his beautiful mouth, "she had to work again last night."

"That might explain *her* taking off in such a hurry, but not why you went with her—unless she needed help getting into her uniform!"

"Watch your mouth!" he said, but there was no bite in his words, and when he turned his glance on Lily, it seemed to rest on her longer than necessary and with particular warmth, before he continued, "I had some matters to attend to in town. Phone calls to make."

"On a Saturday?" Natalie snorted, disbelievingly.

"They were urgent," he said, helping himself to iced

tea. "As a social worker-in-training, you ought to know better than most that not every problem conveniently arises during normal business hours."

Ignoring Cynthia's frown of disapproval, Natalie planted her elbows on the table and wagged a finger at her brother. "Sebastian, you're hiding something!"

"Why do you say that?"

"Because you're talking like a lawyer and you only ever do that around us when you're up to something. Come on, we're your family. You can tell us. What's going on? Did you dump Penny?"

Again, his gaze drifted over Lily before he answered. "We reached an understanding."

"And...?"

"We agreed to remain friends, but otherwise go our separate ways."

In the babble of comment that followed his news, no one seemed to notice that his eyes locked with Lily's and conveyed a silent message meant only for her. Was she delusional to think he was telling her *she* was the reason? Had the fact that they couldn't keep their hands off each other whenever they were alone dealt a death blow to his other relationship?

His slow smile told her it was so.

"But that doesn't explain why you decided to come back here last night, instead of staying in town," Natalie said.

He laughed. "I think you're chasing the wrong profession, Nat. You should be studying law. You'd make a great prosecutor."

She grimaced. "Quit trying to change the subject."

"I heard there was a storm headed this way and thought I'd better come back in case you ran into trouble out here."

"And thank heavens you did! We were so concerned about the roof leaking that we weren't paying attention to how long Lily had been gone." Cynthia shuddered. "What might have happened to her if you hadn't shown up to rescue her doesn't bear thinking about."

"No, it doesn't," he said, covering Lily's hand.

A warmth stole through her at such an open gesture of affection and for the first time in many months, the hurt she'd carried inside began to ease. Gratefully she looked around the table: at Cynthia who'd welcomed her without reserve; at Natalie with whom the bonds of sistership had grown so strong in such a short time; at Hugo, who'd risked losing her a second time rather than shattering her illusions about Genevieve.

And then, last, first and always, there was Sebastian.

Flustered, she shied away from his glance. She'd lost a very great deal. Jonathan Speirs had cheated her and because of him, she'd been subjected to embarrassing cross-examination by the police. But she'd held fast in her belief in the justice system and emerged in the end with her reputation intact.

Her parents were dead, they hadn't always been quite the perfect people she'd believed them to be, and they'd lied to her, even if only by omission. But they'd given far more than they'd ever taken away.

Never be afraid to follow your heart, her mother had said. *It's the one thing that will never lead you astray.*

Nor had it. Instead it had brought her to this moment. To her destiny. She'd been avoiding facing the obvious for days, but suddenly it overwhelmed her and refused to go ignored any longer. She'd fallen in love with Sebastian Caine. Often difficult, at times *impossible,* he was the only man for her. She knew it as surely as she knew her own name.

As if the same realization had crept up on him, too, he squeezed her fingers and she looked up to find him smiling at her with that special intimacy shared only by lovers. Perhaps Hugo and Cynthia saw what was happening, but were too discreet to comment openly.

Natalie showed no such restraint. "Uh-oh! I smell romance in the air," she crowed.

Although meaning no harm, her throwing something so new and untried under public scrutiny ruined the moment. Hot with embarrassment, Lily pulled her hand free and sprang away from the table.

"Honestly, Nat, talk about nineteen going on five!" Sebastian exploded, glaring at his sister with rare annoyance. "When are you going to grow up?"

Obviously crushed, she muttered, "Sorry. I was only teasing. I didn't think—"

"You never do, that's the trouble! Your mouth's in gear long before your brain's engaged!"

"Perhaps," Hugo said, obviously hoping to defuse the tension, which threatened to turn a pleasant get-together into a family free-for-all, "it's time we thought about heading back to town. Last night was long and trying for all of us, and I know I'm feeling the effects today."

"Good idea." Cynthia dabbed her napkin to her mouth and stood up. "If everyone's had enough to eat, I'll start clearing away these dishes."

Ignoring Natalie, Sebastian came to where Lily had drifted to the end of the porch overlooking the lake. "I'm sorry about that, Lily. I don't know what came over Nat. The last thing I wanted was for you to be made to feel uncomfortable."

"It was as much my fault as hers," she said quickly. "If I hadn't overreacted the way I did, we'd all have had a good laugh and that would have been the end of it. Look at her, Sebastian. She's devastated.''

''She'll get over it. And don't blame yourself. She pulls this kind of thoughtless stunt too often and I meant what I said. She *does* need to grow up.'' He stepped close enough that his breath stirred wisps of hair on her forehead. ''Will you drive back to town with me, Lily? There's something I need to talk to you about—a lot of things, in fact.''

The urgency in his voice struck a chord, and she'd have liked nothing more than to be alone with him so that she could express all that was in her heart, too. But, ''It's more important that you straighten things out with Natalie,'' she said. ''Take her with you instead.''

He stood with his back to the others so that when he opened her hand and traced lazy circles over her palm, no one but she was the wiser. ''But you're the one I want to be with.''

Under his heated gaze, happiness swelled inside her like a flower bursting open under the sun. Past tragedy and broken trust left scars. Nothing would ever bring back her parents, or alter the fact that she'd been fooled into entering into a business contract with a criminal.

But with Sebastian looking at her like that, what she'd gained outweighed what she'd lost and she wasn't about to let anything intrude on the perfection of the moment. ''I want to be with you, too, but we're only talking about an hour. Take Natalie, Sebastian, and put things right between you. You and I can see each other later.''

He heaved a sigh. ''It'll have to be a lot later. Hugo mentioned that you're all invited next door to the Andersons' for cocktails this evening. You'll be lucky if you get away from there before nine or ten.''

He was wearing shorts and an open-necked shirt.

Taking advantage of the privacy screen his width of shoulder provided, she slid her fingers between the buttons of his shirt and rested them against his bare chest. "Would you rather wait until tomorrow to get together, then?"

"Keep that up, and you can forget waiting any time at all," he warned her thickly. "I'm likely to put on a floor show right here and now that'll send your father and my mother into orbit, never mind Natalie."

"Perish the thought!" She pursed her lips in a kiss. "So what—?"

"So as soon as you can escape the Andersons, come to the apartment."

"You aren't going to join us for cocktails?"

"Not a chance, sweetheart. I've got a party of my own to organize."

"Semi-dressy," Cynthia told Lily, when she'd asked about the Anderson affair. "Winona isn't one to stand on ceremony, but she likes to do things with style."

Style and elegance pretty much defined everything that took place in the Preston circle of friends, from what Lily could determine. "If I were staying here much longer, I'd need to buy a whole new wardrobe," she muttered, subjecting herself to a last inspection in her bedroom mirror.

The plainly cut black dress with its narrow skirt and fitted waist had seen more than its share of wear lately. But with the addition of a single string of pearls, matching earrings and the pearl dinner ring her parents had given her on her last birthday, she thought it passed muster.

However, the disfavor with which Sebastian regarded her when she finally escaped the cocktail party and at last showed up at his door, made her wonder if it was time she consigned the outfit to a used-clothing store. *Not,* she thought, noting his rather rumpled look, *that he'd have topped anyone's best-dressed list himself just then!*

"Were you sleeping?" she said, dismayed that he confined his greeting to a peck on her cheek and a wordless gesture, which she took to be an invitation for her to climb the winding staircase. "You look a bit...out of sorts."

He shook his head. "Merely anxious to clear up a few things."

But the warmth he'd shown earlier was lacking, and instead of heralding anticipation, his words seemed to clang with foreboding.

"Want something to drink?" he inquired offhandedly, when they reached the living room.

"Thanks. Perrier, if you have it," she said, not liking the situation at all. It reminded her too much of the only other time she'd been a guest in his home, except that, then, she'd wanted information and he'd been bent on seduction. Now it seemed to be the other way around.

"So, how was the cocktail party?"

"Very nice."

He served her drink and waved her to a seat on the same couch where they'd first made love, but seemed in no hurry to join her. Yet just that morning, his every gesture and glance had indicated he was eager to explore the romantic dimensions of their relationship. "Meet any new people?"

"A few. No one interesting enough to keep me there a moment longer than necessary," she said, her glance roaming over the room. No moonlight tonight to bathe it in mystery. No candles, either, or soft music filling the air, or imported wine chilling in ice.

Yet, *I've got a party of my own to organize,* he'd said, when she'd asked him why he wasn't going to the Andersons'. But although the halogen lamp spilling light on the papers spread over his desk was unquestionably efficient, it hardly made for romantic ambience. At their present rate of nonprogress, he'd be showing her the door before much longer with nothing resolved between them.

Well, she wouldn't allow it! Not when they'd come this far, and not until he'd aired whatever was preying on his mind! "What's wrong, Sebastian?" she said, placing her glass on the coffee table and going to where he stood by the window. "Is it Natalie? She begged off coming with us tonight, claiming she had to catch up on her studying, but I thought she seemed a bit down. Are the two of you still on the outs with each other over this morning's incident?"

"No," he said, the look he turned on her about as warm as April in Antarctica. "Thanks to you, we're fighting about something else."

"Me?" She almost laughed. "What have I done now?"

"Oh, plenty, not the least being your latest interference in this family's affairs! Just who do you think you are, encouraging her to take off on some wild-goose chase to India?"

"So that's what this is all about! I gather you don't like the idea very much?"

"No, I do not."

Still not able to take him too seriously despite his black scowl, she said, "Well, the last I heard, it's okay for people to disagree sometimes, Sebastian. It doesn't make them sworn enemies."

"This amounts to more than a disagreement. We're talking about my sister here—a nineteen-year-old girl who thinks the sun rises and sets on every damn thing you say or do. And I don't like the influence you're exerting over her. I'm beginning to think I was right in the first place—

we'd all have been a sight better off if you'd never come here.''

''I think you're exaggerating,'' she said, her earlier hopes and optimism suddenly seeming as absurdly far-fetched as her misplaced amusement. If something this trivial could so easily derail them, perhaps they weren't quite as firmly set on the rosy path to romance, after all. ''You're her idol, Sebastian, not I, and your influence far exceeds anything I might have to say. But do go on with your diatribe. I can hardly wait to hear the rest of it.''

''Lately it's what you think that carries the most weight with Natalie. In my book, that means you're obligated to show some responsibility for the advice you dish out.'' Nostrils pinched with annoyance, he glared at her, the almighty Sebastian Caine conveying displeasure to a lowly subject. ''You had no right encouraging her to put herself in danger.''

And to think she'd been ready to lay her heart on the line for him!

''Don't be ridiculous,'' she snapped, all the old hostility surging to life with renewed vigor. ''Natalie's going to Bombay with a team of professionals to work with un-derprivileged children, not setting out alone to conquer Everest. You need to get a sense of proportion here, Sebastian!''

''When I want your advice, I'll ask for it.''

''I'll be sure to remember that,'' she said. ''Meanwhile, Natalie *did* ask for my advice, and I gave it to her.''

''Where are your brains, for God's sake? You've seen firsthand how immature she still is—how she acts like a kid, half the time.''

''I agree. Unlike you, though, I don't see that as an indication of impaired mental ability. Natalie's bright, in-telligent and eager to learn. And I happen to think this special project will go a long way toward helping her grow up.''

She headed toward the stairs, as eager to be gone as she had been to arrive. Whatever sweet promise the evening had held had long since evaporated. She thought he'd accepted her place in the family but it was obvious she was as much an outsider as ever. "At least give me credit for being up-front and open about it. I didn't go sneaking around behind your back."

"Not this time, perhaps."

She flung an outraged glance over her shoulder. "Exactly what's that supposed to mean?"

"Oh, can the innocent act, Lily! It's pretty ludicrous, coming from someone who's been covering up ever since the day she set foot in this town. It strikes me, from the mess you left behind in Vancouver, that you'd be better off attending to your own business and leaving other people to mind theirs."

"What do you know about my life in Vancouver?" she asked, a stillness draping over her like a cold, wet cloak.

"More than I care to," he shot back. "I've known for days that your flower shop's been closed down and you're under suspicion of fraud and conspiracy. Now I learn your business cohort has links with organized crime. Nice company you keep, Lily! Just the kind of people Hugo and my mother would love to invite into their home and include in their social circle! What I don't know is when you were going to share all these sordid facts with the family you claim is so important to you."

Shock rendered her temporarily speechless. Staggering slightly, she steadied herself against the back of the couch and finally said, "Never, if I could help it! I'm not proud of having been so gullible and stupid."

"But not so ashamed that you stayed out of our lives!"

"I didn't say I was ashamed. I'm not! I don't know where you got your information, but if you'd—"

"I'm a lawyer, in case you've forgotten. I know how to dig up dirt on people. All it took was a phone call to the right party to set things in motion."

"You hired a private detective to spy on me?" she whispered, all the lovely warm certainty that, with him, she'd found her soul mate, shriveling up and dying.

"That's putting it a little fancifully, but it more or less fits the description. I had your background investigated."

"When?"

"Within days of your getting here, but it's been an ongoing project." He strode to the desk and tried to shove a sheet of paper into her hand. "I received the latest report just this afternoon. Read it for yourself."

"I don't care to!" She slapped it aside, furious, dismayed and, most of all, deeply hurt. She'd been willing to trust this man with her heart! For her to discover now that, all the time he was seducing her so expertly, he'd had another agenda…!

She felt as if she'd been hit, hard. She felt battered and bruised and torn to shreds inside. "Do you know why I came here tonight?" she said, in a low, broken voice. "Because I wanted to tell you that I love you. Because I thought you were going to say the same thing to me."

"The idea had crossed my mind." He looked as haggard as she felt. "I guess it just goes to show what self-delusional fools we can be sometimes."

"I trusted you!"

"I wish I could say the same about you."

"You could. *Can!* If you'd just asked me, instead of—"

"Every day that passed, I waited for you to say something. Hoped you'd have the decency to come clean and

tell me the kind of trouble you're in. Hoped the next report I received would clear your name. But you remained
silent, and the investigator kept turning up more dirt, cul-
minating in today's report. Sorry, Lily, but that doesn't
exactly inspire trust.''

She could have pleaded her case. But why waste her
time?

''I won't bother trying to justify my actions,'' she said,
holding her head high. ''You've already judged and found
me guilty. I'm sure you'd find my protestations of inno-
cence laughable.''

''The evidence against you is pretty conclusive. You
can hardly blame me for being concerned.''

''There *is* no evidence against me!'' she spat. ''Or if
there is, it's entirely circumstantial, a concept you appear
to have dismissed out of hand. But from where I stand,
there's certainly plenty against you.''

''Oh, really?'' He sneered, supremely confident of his
superiority, his unimpeachable moral fiber. Clearly it had
never occurred to him the rest of the world might view
him as just a little less than perfect. ''Such as what?''

''You're not the man I took you to be, Sebastian Caine,
and I am *so* glad you showed your true colors before I
made an even bigger fool of myself than I already have.
You've been determined to discredit me from the minute
you set eyes on me. As for your righteous indignation
about my sins of omission, you could certainly give me
lessons in underhandedness!''

He looked vaguely disturbed by her vehemence.
''Hey,'' he said, spreading his hands palms up, as if he
were the most reasonable creature on earth, and she nothing but a woman in the throes of PMS or some other kind
of hormonal imbalance, ''if there's something I've missed

in all this, fill me in. Defend yourself. I'm willing to listen. I always have been.''

''Why waste my breath? You've already got enough ammunition to condemn me out of hand. I'm able to spend unlimited time here because I don't have a job waiting for me in Vancouver. Why? Because the police closed down my business. And why was that, you ask? Because it was a cover-up for organized crime, which naturally makes me some sort of Mafia gun moll. So why did I show up here? Because Daddy's rich as well as good-looking, and so full of guilt at having abandoned me that touching him up for money to bail myself out of my current mess will be a piece of cake for an experienced crook like me.''

Running out of steam, she pressed a hand to her chest and drew in a fresh lungful of air. ''Good grief, Sebastian, how much more proof do you need that you've jumped to all the right conclusions?''

''Just hold your fire a second,'' he said, advancing toward her. ''Something here doesn't—''

''No! I've heard enough. More than enough! You want me out of your life? You've got it! I'm gone! You'll never have to breathe the same air as me again. As far as I'm concerned, Sebastian Caine, you're history that's well on the way to being permanently forgotten. But just so there's no misunderstanding, I'm not giving up on Natalie or Hugo. They're all the family I've got left, and I'll see you in hell before I let you shove me out of their lives, as well.''

Seeing him winding up to argue the point, she spun on her high heels and took off down the narrow, winding stairs with dangerous disregard for her safety. She'd rather have broken her neck than give him the chance to have the last word.

"Tomorrow," she promised herself, sprinting as best she could through the shrubbery and across the lawns to the main house, "I'll be on the first flight out of here, if I have to charter a private jet to do it. I'll gather enough proof to show him just how far off the mark he is with his nasty suspicions! Before I'm done with him, he'll wind up with so much egg on his face that no one will recognize him!"

Hugo hauled him on the carpet the next afternoon. Or, more accurately, he showed up at the law firm, something he hadn't done in months, and after being admitted to Sebastian's office, closed the door behind him with a quiet precision that broadcast his displeasure loud and clear.

"Lily left town this morning," he began, without preamble. "And it didn't take a genius to figure out that she was very upset. You told her, didn't you? Against my express wishes, you told her the truth about her mother."

Sebastian held him with too much respect and affection to take the easy way out. "Yes, I did. Quite a long time ago. That's not why she's gone, but you're right in assuming I'm responsible for her leaving." He looked his stepfather straight in the eye. "I initiated an investigation into her past, also against your express wishes, and she found out about it."

Hugo sagged in his chair, suddenly looking all of his seventy years. "Why, Sebastian? By what right did you take it upon yourself to invade her privacy like that?"

He'd asked himself the same question a thousand times since she'd stormed out of his apartment. "Damned if I really know," he said. "In the beginning, I suppose I was looking out for you, protecting you. You were so trusting, so ready to take her at face value. I wanted to make sure you weren't going to wind up being hurt, that she wasn't a chip off the old block, out to take advantage of you. At first, all I intended was to confirm she was who and what she claimed to be, but it got out of hand...." He heaved a sigh. "Stuff turned up that put her in a pretty bad light and I felt I had to keep going. If it makes any difference, Hugo, I was hoping my source would unearth something that would clear her."

"Damn it, Sebastian!" Hugo was white around the mouth, his eyes blazing. Normally a man of temperate nature, he was formidable when roused to anger. Sebastian could count on one hand the number of times he'd witnessed it. "I've been in the legal profession a long time and I consider myself a pretty sound judge of people. I don't need proof of Lily's good character. But I am beyond disappointed in you."

Sebastian pushed away from the desk and paced across the carpet. "I'm pretty disappointed in me, too. During our last conversation, I told her I didn't trust her, but the truth is, I don't trust myself around her. She clouds my judgment, Hugo. She makes all the boundaries marking my life shift out of focus. I pride myself on being a man willing to be held accountable for his actions, yet where she's concerned, I break all the rules that normally govern my conduct."

"Are you telling me you think you're in love with her?" Hugo swiveled in his chair and subjected him to a disconcertingly probing gaze.

Jeez, if that were his only sin! But he'd had to compound his errors by making love to her. He'd had sex with his stepfather's daughter, for God's sake! What kind of jerk was he that, even now, visions of her lying hot and naked beneath him colored his mind and evoked the taste and scent of her with startling clarity?

"I think," he said, choosing his words carefully because, for the first time ever, he couldn't be completely honest with the man who'd guided him into manhood with unwavering dedication, "that any such possibility was nipped in the bud last night."

"So that's it, then." Wearily Hugo got to his feet. "I had hoped our perfect summer might last indefinitely. Instead both my daughters are flying the coop."

"Both?"

"Natalie leaves for India at the end of next week."

"I can't believe you've agreed to letting her go. Hugo, I really don't think that's a smart idea."

"You'll forgive me, Sebastian," came the reply, "if I don't hold your opinion in much regard right now. You chose to interfere in my relationship with Lily. I'm not disposed to let you do the same where Natalie's concerned. Your mother and I both feel this is an opportunity unlikely to come her way again and are encouraging her to take full advantage of it."

The silence he left behind rang with recrimination. *I've screwed up,* Sebastian thought gloomily. *And I've done it in spectacular fashion.*

The question was, how could he redeem himself, not only in Hugo's eyes, but, more importantly, in his own?

CHAPTER TEN

HE KNEW the answer, of course. And if he hadn't been able to figure it out for himself, the final investigative report arriving on his desk five days later spelled out in conclusive detail the extent to which he'd misjudged Lily. No question about it: he was going to have to swallow *all* his pride, not just selected parts.

He waited until Natalie was safely en route to her adventure and he'd cleared his desk of his most urgent cases before telling his mother and Hugo of his plans. "I'm flying out to B.C. next week. I could phone, and save myself the time and trouble of making the trip, but I figure I owe it to Lily to deliver my apology in person. I'm booked into the Hotel Vancouver if you need to reach me."

"How long will you be gone?" Cynthia asked.

"As long as it takes." He looked at Hugo. "I don't really expect her to forgive me, but I hope, in time, you can."

"I've looked on you as a son for a good number of years, Sebastian," Hugo said. "It'll take more than one mistake on your part for that to change."

He should have found the words comforting but, as he left his mother and stepfather standing on the terrace, he felt only ashamed and strangely uneasy. Suddenly they both looked old and very alone.

He was not a man given to superstition, yet the apprehension stayed with him all during the long flight west the next day. He hoped Lily would agree to see him that

157

night, that he could persuade her to return with him to Stentonbridge as soon as possible, and spend what remained of the summer with her family.

He didn't phone ahead to warn her of his visit, figuring he'd be better off taking her by surprise. The way he saw it, that was probably his only chance of getting her to open her door to him.

She lived on the top floor of a fourteen story apartment building overlooking English Bay. It was growing dark when he arrived, and not much was left of the sunset but an orange glow behind the mountains on the far side of Georgia Strait.

He stationed himself in an inconspicuous spot among the potted palms screening the foyer from the street, certain he wouldn't have long to wait before someone opened the main entrance and he could slip inside the building.

What he hadn't counted on was that that person would be Lily. She came running up the steps from the street not five minutes later, with a sack of groceries swinging from her hand and what looked like a French baguette in a bag tucked under her arm.

She had no idea she was being watched, no sense that he was right behind her, until he touched her on the shoulder as she juggled her purchases and tried to fit her key into the lock. He thought he was prepared for her possible reaction at seeing him again—anything from her slamming his foot in the door to trying to shove him down the nearest stairwell. But her subdued shriek of alarm and the way the groceries flew out of her hand and hit the ground with a resounding *thwack* startled him almost as much as he'd obviously startled her.

"Hey," he said, patting her soothingly, "it's just me."

"*Just* you?" she echoed faintly, clutching the French bread to her bosom and turning huge, fear-filled eyes on him. "That makes it even worse than what I originally expected. What are you doing here, lurking in the bushes like some pervert?"

"Waiting to talk to you. Are you going to invite me upstairs, or shall we sit on the steps out here?"

"Neither," she said. "And stop patting me as if you were trying to placate a vicious dog."

"Nervous, perhaps, but never vicious," he said rue-fully, unable to take his eyes off her. Agitation stained her cheeks a rosy pink and left her breasts heaving delec-tably under her lightweight summer dress. Swallowing, he bent down and stuffed a carton of peach ice cream, a bag of frozen French fries, a king-size bottle of ketchup, and a box of chocolate-covered peanuts into the grocery sack. "Still a junk-food goddess, I see," he said, handing it over.

"Not that it's any of your business, but yes. Some of us really are what we first appear to be."

Uh-oh, the way things were shaping up didn't look promising! "Look, Lily, you don't owe me a damn thing—"

"How magnanimous of you!"

"And if you insist, I won't push you to hear me out. But I've come a long way, in more ways than one, since we last spoke, so I'm asking you, please, to let me try to put a few things right." He stepped closer, hemming her into the narrow space between the intercom panel and the front door. "Please?"

"Don't you dare touch me," she warned, wielding the bread like a sword. "I don't ever want you to touch me again!"

"That's a pity," he said softly, "because I find myself wanting to touch you very badly. But it's not my primary reason for being here."

"Then what is?"

He glanced around. "Do we really have to go into it here? Isn't there someplace more private we can talk—a coffee shop or a hotel lounge?"

"I've got perishables that need to be refrigerated," she said, eyeing him narrowly. "You can come up to my apartment and I'll give you ten minutes to say your piece, then you're out of here."

Her home was spacious and as elegantly understated as she herself. "Lovely view you've got," he remarked, strolling to the balcony and looking over the treetops to the curving shoreline below.

"Ten minutes, Sebastian," she reminded him, stashing her stuff in the streamlined kitchen. "So never mind the small talk."

"Okay." He pivoted to face her. "I've been a damned fool. I know I treated you shabbily. I should have trusted you, taken you at your word—at face value, as you once said. You're furious with me, and I don't blame you. And I want you to know I'm sorry."

"Are you really? And what brought about this massive change of heart?" she inquired coldly. "Could it have something to do with the fact that you've finally got the goods on my oh-so-shady past, and now have proof I'm not the reincarnation of Lizzie Borden, after all?"

"Well, I—"

"Don't bother denying it, Sebastian. You're not the only legal eagle on the planet with connections. The minute I got back to Vancouver, I contacted my lawyer and let her know exactly what you'd been up to. She flushed out your weasely little sleuth in no time flat and he, in turn, relayed to you everything he subsequently learned from her—which is that I'm really quite harmless and have no evil designs on any of the people you guard so jealously.''

"All true, every word," he said. "And I apologize for having ever doubted you."

"And is that all you came to say?"

He'd thought he could manage the rest. Admit that he hadn't been able to get her out of his mind. Tell her that she…that he…that what he felt for her amounted to…

Love: the most straightforward four-letter word in the world, and the most difficult to say, lodged in his throat and he couldn't spit it out. Instead he hedged the question with pompous, pointless evasions that he knew weren't what she wanted to hear. "It's the most important thing, certainly. I take no pleasure in having judged you so harshly."

"Well, hope that God can forgive you," she said, "because I can't. I'm not interested in an apology made after the fact. You didn't believe in me when it counted, Sebastian, and I don't need your support now."

"Jeez!" he said, frustration getting the better of him in the face of her obstinacy. "You're not entirely blameless in all this, you know, coming across as the poor orphaned little waif in mourning one minute, then parading around the next with enough clothes and jewelry stashed in your wardrobe to keep a countess on a world tour well dressed!"

"Well, excuse me! If I'd known *that* was a concern, I'd have shown you a copy of my parents' will and you could have seen for yourself that I've been left rather well-off. But even if I hadn't inherited a penny, I was never the money-grubbing impostor out to punish an old man by fleecing him of every penny, the way you implied I was. So take your injured pride and stuff it, Sebastian, along with your apology! My name and reputation are

squeaky clean and I intend to pick up my life and go on—
without your blessing, thank you very much.''

"You know," he said, stung by her absolute disdain,
''you could have prevented a lot of this unpleasantness if
you'd just come clean in the beginning. Why the hell
didn't you at least confide in me about your business problems?''

"Because I'd done nothing wrong! And I shouldn't
have to tell you that, in this country at least, a person is
deemed innocent until proven guilty.''

"No," he said heavily. "In the end, of course, it does
all come down to that, doesn't it, and saying I'm sorry
hardly compensates.''

"Hardly," she said, snippily enough that his temper
rose again.

"What *would* you like, then? My head on a platter?''

She regarded him across the width of the kitchen, her
color still high, and her beautiful eyes suddenly empty.
Despite all the things that had gone wrong between them,
one thing had always been right: their lovemaking had
been touched with rare perfection. He could have tried to
recapture that special magic, but he knew it was no longer
enough.

"Nothing quite that dramatic," she said dully, "and
certainly nothing you're not able to offer willingly.''

"You're not making this easy, Lily!''

"Deceiving someone who trusted you isn't supposed to
be easy, Sebastian, so if you don't like where it's landed
you, go cry on someone else's shoulder. And show yourself out, while you're at it. Your time's up.''

Baffled, he swung away from that flat, empty gaze. "I
know what you want to hear, but be reasonable, for Pete's
sake! Don't ask me to rush blindly into something I'm
only just coming to terms with.''

"Why not? You had no hesitation about rushing blindly into bed with me while your paid flunky ran a check to make sure I deserved to be welcomed into the bosom of your precious family."

"Isn't it enough that I've missed you every second you've been gone? That when I saw you tonight, what I most wanted was to take you in my arms? Can't that be enough for now?"

"No," she said, stalking to the door and flinging it open. "I've already got plenty of friends more than happy to wrap their arms around me if a feel-good hug is what I need to see me through the night. I'm sorry you came all this way for nothing."

Considering she stood nine inches shorter and weighed at least eighty pounds less than he did, she hustled him out of the apartment with astonishing speed. "Hey!" he roared, his male pride mortally offended. "I'm not finished!"

"Oh, yes, you are," she replied, from the other side of the door.

He debated thundering on the blasted thing with his fist. Better yet, aiming a good kick and smashing in the lock. But he'd made enough mistakes where she was concerned, and he'd be damned if he'd compound them by giving her the pleasure of calling the police and having him hauled off to jail for the night. He'd accomplished what he'd set out to do.

As for what didn't get done—the emotional stuff that snuck up whenever he found himself within kissing distance of her—well, that had never been part of the original game plan and a man of his experience ought to know better than to switch strategies halfway through. The day had yet to dawn when Sebastian Caine became a fool for love.

*   *   *

Long after he'd stomped off, she remained plastered to the door, her heart beating such a furious tattoo that she wasn't at all sure she could make it to the nearest chair without going into cardiac arrest.

She'd dreamed about him day and night in the weeks since she'd walked out of his life. A hundred times or more, she'd thought she'd seen him on a crowded Vancouver street, on the beach at dusk, across a noisy restaurant during the lunch hour. The set of a pair of broad shoulders, the angle of a stranger's dark head, a graceful, long-legged masculine stride—how often had wishful thinking led her astray?

Memory had deceived her, too. The motel where they'd spent their first night had been indescribably tacky, yet, in retrospect, became a magical place where the beginnings of a love affair had sprung to life. The scent of him, the olive tint of his skin turned darker where the sun had touched it, his thigh brushing hers in the night, his breath ruffling her hair…oh, if only she'd known how it would all end!

Ironically he'd been the last thing on her mind tonight as she'd walked home from the supermarket. Hearing earlier that her former business associate had signed a confession, which spared her the ordeal of having to testify against him in court, had lifted such a weight off her shoulders that she'd been almost happy.

Then she'd turned and found Sebastian there, warm and solid and real, and wild hope had sprung to life. But she'd been fooled again. All he'd wanted was to ease his conscience with an apology and the bonus of a little sex thrown in on the side, whereas she…

Your heart! she'd wanted to cry out, when he'd asked her what it was she wanted. *Your love—as unconditionally as I'd give you mine, if I thought you'd accept it!*

But there'd never been anything unconditional about his feelings for her, and no use fooling herself otherwise. Even when he shuddered in her arms, and his seed spilled hot and urgent inside her, and he kissed her as if his life depended on it, he held a part of himself back.

He might find her desirable, but he'd never found her irresistible, and she was smart enough not to settle for anything less. Because, she wanted *him*. All of him! Forever!

Why did he have to be so beautiful, so persuasive, so stunningly sexy? And what in the world was wrong with her, that she was crying like a baby over a man who didn't deserve her tears?

"Sending him away was the only thing to do," she wailed to the kitchen at large as she spread frozen French fries on a cookie tray and popped them into the oven. If ever she needed comfort food, it was tonight! "Count your blessings, you silly twit. You're luckier than most people who lose their parents too soon. You found a new family—a father and a sister, and a lovely stepmother. Don't ask for the moon, as well."

In the weeks that followed, the phone calls from Hugo and Cynthia, and the postcards from Natalie were what kept her grounded. If Sebastian came sneaking into her thoughts when she wasn't looking, a flurry of late-summer weddings kept her busy enough to shunt him aside, and she had Thanksgiving in early October to look forward to. Natalie would be back from India by then, and had promised to fly out to spend the holiday weekend in Vancouver with her.

The call came on the first Friday in October. After work, she'd gone shopping for pretty new sheets for the guest room, in preparation for her sister's arrival the following Thursday, and didn't get home until well after sunset. When she opened her front door, the first thing she saw was the red blinking light on her telephone answering machine.

Hugo's voice was so low and distraught that she was hard-pressed to make out his words and had to play the message over again before she caught the gist of it. "Lily, it's your...it's Hugo. We've received some bad news, I'm afraid. Please call me at home."

Sebastian! was her first thought. *Something had happened to Sebastian!*

But when she pressed the Redial button and the phone was picked up at the other end, it was Sebastian who answered.

She had wondered, if or when they spoke again, how she'd find the words; had, ridiculously, practiced what she might say—flippant, glib, meaningless remarks designed to let him know how unimportant he was to her life. How she'd managed to toss him aside. Now that the moment was at hand, though, she simply spoke from the heart.

"Oh, Sebastian, thank God you're all right! It's me, Lily. I just got Hugo's message. What's happened? Has there been an accident?"

"No." She had never believed anything could defeat this man she loved so well despite herself; never believed he could know despair. Hearing both in his voice now terrified her. "It's Natalie, Lily. She's...very ill."

"Ill, how?" she cried. "I spoke to her just the other day, and she was fine. *Fine!* There must be some mistake."

"Oh, there was a mistake, all right, and it happened the day she got on that flight to India," he said bitterly. "If she'd listened to me and stayed home—!"

"What's India got to do with anything? She came home over two weeks ago. She's resumed her university studies.

She was happy and healthy and coming to visit me in another few days.''

She hadn't recognized the shrill edge of panic in her voice, but trust him to waste no time setting her straight. "Get a grip, Lily! We've got enough to deal with, without your falling apart. Natalie's come down with some sort of post-infection complication from some bug she picked up in Bombay, and it's not responding to treatment. She's been hospitalized and her doctors are very worried. I'm afraid it's looking very serious. Unless things turn around, her life could be in danger.''

The strength went out of Lily's legs and she fell into the nearest chair like a rag doll. *He was implying that vital, irreverent, lovely young woman with so much living to do might die!* "Don't say that!" she wailed. "Don't even dare to *think* it!"

"I'm sorry, Lily. I know what a shock this is. We're all walking around in a daze. Going through the motions. Waiting for a miracle.''

"I'm coming out," she said, her thoughts scrambling to catch up and make sense of such a senseless tragedy. "I'll be there as soon as I can.''

"Why? There's nothing you can do.''

"Because she's my sister and I want to be with her! And you're not going to talk me out of it, so don't even try!''

His tone softened, and a weariness crept in that brought tears to her eyes. "Let me know when you're due to arrive and I'll meet your flight.''

The last time they'd sped through the gentle, rolling countryside, the roads had been awash with mud, the flowers in the gardens flattened from the rain. This time, the weather was indecently lovely. The leaves splashed red and gold against the soft blue sky. Chrysanthemums and purple asters lined pathways leading to cottage doors; scarlet geraniums nestled in window boxes.

She had barely slept since hearing the news. Most of the time, worry had occupied her mind. During the brief moments that she had been able to turn her thoughts elsewhere, she'd wondered how it would be, seeing Sebastian again. Except for fighting or making love, they'd had so little practice in interacting. But when she saw him waiting at the airport, she'd started to cry and they'd simply walked into each other's arms and held on to each other in wordless grief.

"How is she?" she finally asked him, as the miles spun by and the silence became too oppressive to bear. "Any change?"

"None."

"Is there no cure? No treatment?"

His chest rose in a massive sigh and he had to clear his throat before answering. "Her doctors are trying everything they've got."

Lily smothered a sob. "How did things come to this ugly pass, Sebastian? What went wrong so suddenly?"

"She picked up a strep infection in Bombay. Although she was treated with appropriate antibiotics and seemed to make a normal recovery at the time, complications set in which didn't become apparent until recently, and now her kidneys are affected."

He closed his eyes briefly, and she thought she'd never seen him look so desolate. Reaching over, she covered his hand as it rested on the gearshift. At her touch, he curled his fingers around hers and didn't let go. "I'm glad you're here," he said brusquely. "Hugo needs you, and so do I."

Why did it take tragedy to bring us together? she wondered sadly. *Why couldn't we have found trust and solace in each other before?*

"It's a rare disorder," he went on, after a few seconds. "Only about one in ten thousand comes down with it, and the vast majority usually do respond to treatment which, from what I understand, is largely confined to relieving symptoms. But every once in a while, more serious complications set in—congestive heart failure, hypertension or, in this case and unfortunately for Nat, kidney problems. The medical term for her condition is poststreptococcal glomerulonephritis, which is a mouthful by anyone's standards. Simply translated, it means the capillaries in the kidneys become inflamed and don't filter and excrete the way they should."

"People can't function without healthy kidneys," she said, cold fingers of dread crawling up her spine. "They..."

He understood exactly which path her thoughts were following. "If the condition can't be reversed, she'll need a transplant. If a compatible donor isn't found..."

His voice cracked, betraying the misery and dread he was working so hard to conceal. Devastated for everyone but, at that moment, especially for him, Lily fought to control her own fears. "Oh, Sebastian, I know how frightening this must be for all of you and I wish there was something I could do to make it more bearable."

"There isn't. Family means everything to me and the idea that I could lose my sister...!" Wrenching his emotions under control, he squeezed Lily's fingers. "But your being here will be of some comfort to Hugo, I know."

But I want to comfort you, too, she longed to tell him. *I want you to turn to me, instead of shutting me out.*

They reached the outskirts of Stentonbridge just before eight o'clock. A faint mist rose from the river, smoke curled toward the stars from the chimneys of the lovely old houses, and the smell of autumn filled the air.

"I'll drop you off and leave you to get settled," Sebastian said, turning through the elegant iron gates and up the sweeping driveway to the Preston estate. "Afraid the only ones to welcome you this time are Katie and the housekeeper, but you know your way around, so make yourself at home. My mother and Hugo will probably stay at the hospital again tonight."

"And what about you?"

"I'm going back there, too."

"Not without me, you aren't," she said. "The chief reason I'm here is to see Natalie."

He inhaled sharply, always a telltale sign that he was irritated. "I've been away all afternoon as it is, Lily. I'm not hanging around while you unpack. I want to be with my sister."

"As do I," she declared, "so instead of wasting time arguing over something we're in agreement on for a change, let's go."

"I hope you're prepared for what's waiting," he said grimly, stepping on the accelerator and speeding off again. "Nat's not the same person you last saw."

Regular visiting hours were over by the time they arrived, and the hallways were filled with that special kind of hush peculiar to hospitals at night. In the Intensive Care Unit, though, people wandered distractedly up and down the waiting area, their faces tight and anxious.

A nurse stopped them as Sebastian led Lily through a set of double doors to the main area. "Glad you got here when you did, Mr. Caine," she said quietly. "Your sister's condition has worsened, I'm afraid, and her doctors are consulting with her parents now." She indicated a small room to one side. "They're in there, if you'd like to join them."

"Is no one with my sister?"

"Not at the moment, though she is, of course, being closely monitored."

He turned to Lily and she saw the question in his eyes. "I'll sit with her," she said. "You go hear what the doctors are saying."

"Thank you. I should be there."

So should I, she thought desolately. *But even at a time like this, you still don't consider me a real part of this family, Sebastian. I'm here on sufferance only.*

But the time to press the point was not now. What mattered was Natalie and she lay so still on the narrow, white bed, with so many tubes stuck in her body, and with a face so waxen and sallow, that Lily feared, when she first laid eyes on her, that she'd come too late.

"Don't be afraid," the same nurse told her, guiding her to a chair beside the bed. "The equipment looks scary, but for now it's doing its job, and that's what counts."

Sebastian had warned her, but nothing could have prepared Lily for the shock. Unable to reconcile present reality with the memory of Natalie as she'd last seen her—laughing, teasing, filled with a zest for life, poised on the brink of a great adventure, bursting with good health and vitality—she whispered brokenly, "She will get better, won't she?"

"We hope so, but it won't hurt to pray for a miracle." The nurse patted her shoulder kindly. "Talk to her. Let her know you're here and that you love her."

"So there you have it. We hope it doesn't come to that, but it's best to be prepared. A transplant might be our only option." The head of the medical team shook his head sympathetically.

Sebastian looked at his mother, at Hugo. Despair and grief had etched new lines on their faces. Instead of young-at-heart seniors, he saw old people, too broken and frail to cope. If Nat died, they would not be long following her. Well, damn it, he wouldn't let it happen, not as long as he had breath left in his body! "And you're absolutely certain I can't be a donor?"

"You know the answer, Mr. Caine. We've run the tests, you've seen the results. Even if you'd been full siblings, there was always the chance you wouldn't be a match. As it is…" The doctor lifted his shoulders in a tired, helpless shrug, as if he'd told the same story to too many other families.

"And us?" Hugo asked. "Her mother and I—?"

"I'm afraid it's out of the question, sir. Any other medical considerations aside, your age is against you."

"I want you to alert every hospital on this continent," Sebastian said, struggling to contain the anger choking him. "Farther than that, in fact. Europe, Asia, Australia, South America. I'll personally charter a plane anywhere in the world and pay whatever it costs to get a healthy kidney here in time, if one should be needed."

"Before you go that far, there is another option," Lily announced from the doorway. Her eyes met his and he saw that she'd been crying. But her gaze and voice held steady. "I want to be tested as a possible donor."

"Oh, my dear!" his mother wept. "Oh, Lily, thank you!"

"My darling daughter, you've already given us so much. And now this…" Hugo struggled to his feet.

"No!" Sebastian said. "You will not do this, Lily!"

"And why not?" she said. "Natalie's my sister, too. You didn't hesitate to offer her one of your kidneys. Why wouldn't I be willing to do the same?"

"Because," he said.

She lifted her eyebrows in mild reproof. "You're going

to have to do a lot better than that, Sebastian. 'Because' is no answer at all.''

"There are other reasons," he blustered, torn between two unacceptable alternatives. He could not stand idly by and let Nat die, but the thought of Lily... *his* Lily... of her lovely, perfect body being...! "No," he said again. "There has to be another way."

"Perhaps," one of the doctors said, "you all need to sleep on this. It's not a decision to be made lightly, and nothing's going to be done tonight anyway, so I suggest you go home and try to get some rest. People generally don't make the best choices when they're overtired and overstressed. If you're still of the same mind tomorrow," he concluded, addressing his last remark to Lily, "let us know and we'll arrange for you to be tested."

"And if I'm a compatible donor?"

"If it becomes necessary—and I stress that we have not reached that point yet and hopefully never will—you and your sister will be put under the care of a urologist with transplant experience. He will perform the surgery."

"Take Lily home," Hugo said, after the medical team had left. "Your mother and I will stay with Natalie."

"You heard the doctor," Sebastian told him. "We all need to get some rest."

"And you know very well that neither of us will sleep a wink away from this hospital. There are comfortable recliners in the waiting area, with plenty of blankets and pillows. I'll call you the minute there's any change, but our place is here with our child, Sebastian, and I'll rest easier if I know you're taking care of my other daughter."

Oh, he'd take care of her, all right! If it took him all night, he'd dissuade Lily from her impulsive offer. "Okay," he said, "we're out of here. Come on, Lily, I'll drive you home."

CHAPTER ELEVEN

"You've missed the turnoff for the main gates," Lily told him.

They were the first words she'd spoken since they left the hospital. Buried in her own thoughts and knowing he was just as occupied with his, she'd seen no point in trying to engage him in empty conversation.

"I know," he said.

"Why? Where are we going?"

"To my place. I use the rear driveway. It's faster."

She didn't want to go to his place. She was too vulnerable to face the memories it would stir up. "I don't think that's such a good idea, Sebastian."

"If we should be called to the hospital in the middle of the night, we'll make it there a lot faster if I don't have to stop by the main house first to collect you."

Half a mile farther down the road, he swung the car through a set of smaller gates and followed a narrow, tree-lined lane, which ended in a clearing in front of the stables. "Also," he said, switching off the engine and turning to face her, "you and I have to talk."

"Talking never gets us anywhere but into trouble." She pushed her hair away from her face wearily. "And I don't know about you, Sebastian, but I've had just about as much of that as I can take for one day."

"Fine. I'll do the talking and all you have to do is listen." He stepped out of the car and came around to her door. "Come on, Lily. This is no time for us to be on opposite sides. We've got to hang together."

She was too tired to argue and, if truth be told, afraid to be alone. Too many nightmares waited. Stoically she watched while he unloaded her luggage from the trunk, then followed him inside the stables and up the winding staircase.

His apartment had a different feel to it with summer gone. A fire snoozed behind glass doors in the hearth and threw a pale orange glow on the high whitewashed ceiling, and he'd moved the leather couches so that they flanked the hearth. Only one window stood open a crack. Although the view beyond was obscured by night, she could hear the river flowing quietly at the foot of the property and was reminded of the many times she and Natalie had walked Katie along its banks. Everywhere she turned, it seemed, there were memories that brought her nothing but pain.

Sebastian dumped her bags on the landing and went to the armoire. She heard the clink of crystal, the splash of liquid—déjà vu again. "Here," he said, coming to where she'd collapsed on one of the couches. "Stay put and drink this."

Suspiciously she inspected the glass he thrust into her hand. "What is it?"

"Not poison, if that's what you're afraid of. I'm sticking with scotch, but when I knew you were coming back, I laid in a supply of the sherry you like. Come on, Lily, don't make me hold your nose and pour it down your throat. We both need something to fortify us."

"I doubt alcohol's going to do it," she said. "It's a depressant, in case you didn't know, and I'm already feeling low enough." She tried, unsuccessfully, to bury a sigh. "What's involved in donating a kidney, Sebastian?"

He didn't answer. Instead he disappeared through a doorway at the back of the room and a moment later, she heard the sound of pots and pans clattering, followed shortly thereafter by the smell of maple-cured bacon frying.

Sebastian Caine, lawyer and lover, she'd come to know well, but this sudden display of domesticity was something new. Curiosity getting the better of the fatigue that had attacked her limbs the minute she sank into the comfort of the couch, she went to investigate.

Shirtsleeves rolled back to just below the elbow and a dish towel tucked in the waist of his dark gray cords, he was slicing tomatoes at a butcher-block island separating the working half of his kitchen from a small dining nook.

Without bothering to look up from the task, he said, "I thought I told you to stay put."

"I wanted to see your kitchen." She leaned against the doorway. Actually "wilted" was a more apt description as the sherry took effect, spreading a warm, delicious lassitude throughout her body. "Somehow, I never expected you'd have one."

A trace of amusement lightened his expression. "You thought elves came in the night and left food on my doorstep?"

"I suppose I never gave the matter much thought at all. We've always had...other avenues to explore whenever we've been together." She took a sip of the sherry. "You didn't answer my question, Sebastian."

"What question?"

"The one about kidney transplants. You've already looked into it so tell me, what do living donors face?"

He set aside the tomatoes, popped two slices of bread into the toaster and opened the refrigerator. "Sorry I can't offer you French fries," he said, "but I make a pretty mean bacon, lettuce and tomato sandwich. You like mayo on yours?"

"You can put strawberry jam on it, for all I care! Stop evading the question, Sebastian. I refuse to be brushed off like this."

"And I refuse to dwell on something that's not going to happen. Nat's going to recover on her own."

"And if she doesn't, and it turns out she needs a kidney from someone else and you aren't a suitable donor, what then? Are you still going to tell me to go away and be quiet?"

"You never know when to quit, do you, Lily?" he said savagely, slamming a head of lettuce and a jar of mayonnaise on the counter, before kicking closed the refrigerator door. "You just have to keep poking away at a subject until you've exhausted it and everyone connected with it. What will it take to satisfy you?"

"Having you treat me as a family member instead of some interfering pariah would be a good place to start. And receiving reasonable answers to reasonable questions."

"Fine." His shoulders slumped. "You'll undergo blood tests and X rays to determine if you're a healthy prospective donor and immunologically compatible with Nat." The toast popped up. He removed it and put in two more slices of bread. "If you pass that hurdle, you'll go through more lab tests and a final evaluation, including assessment by a social worker to ensure that you're genuinely willing to donate."

"And then?"

He looked up and gave her a blast from those unforgettable blue eyes. "If all systems are go, they'll cut you open and remove a kidney."

He put it like that deliberately, hoping the bluntness of his words would shock her into reconsidering. He should have known better. She'd weathered plenty of storms in the last year. One more wasn't going to defeat her.

"It will be worth it, if that's what it takes to save Natalie's life," she said quietly.

"And what about *your* life?" he raged, grabbing the second batch of toast and slapping it down on the cutting board. "What about the risks you'd be taking, the possible future restrictions you could face with your own health?"

"Life's full of risks, Sebastian. We live with them from the moment we're born. Most of the time, we're able to avoid them, but when someone we love is in trouble, we don't stop to count the cost. We do what we can to help, and if that means taking chances, well…" She shrugged. "We take them. If it turns out that Natalie needs a kidney and I'm able to give her one, I will."

He thought of himself as a man able to take whatever life dished out, but suddenly, he'd reached his limit. He hadn't slept in a week. He'd watched his mother and Hugo age before his eyes. He'd watched Nat slide deeper into illness and never doubted he'd move heaven and earth to make her well again. But he hadn't reckoned on this; on being caught so squarely between a rock and a hard place that he felt as if his heart were being squeezed dry.

Overcome, he swung away and went to lean on the dining table. Planting both hands on its surface, he stared down at them and willed his vision to clear. It would have, too, if Lily hadn't come up behind him and wrapped her arms around his waist, and said, "We are defined by the choices we make, Sebastian. At the end of the day, they are what count."

The words triggered something deep inside him that nothing she'd ever said or done before had quite managed to touch. He'd done his best not to like her, to find good reason to despise her, to forget he'd ever met her. But with those two sentences, she forced him to acknowledge the absolute decency and goodness which were so much a factor in what made her beautiful.

His chest heaved in a silent sob. Part of his mind—the proud, stupid, arrogant part that men swaggered about because it made them feel invincible—reviled him for showing such weakness. But another part gave him the courage to say what had been in his heart for months. "I love you, Lily. Too much to let you do this. Please...don't. *Don't!*"

"It's for Natalie. My sister—*your* sister." She slackened her hold and forced him to turn and face her. "How can you ask me not to do this, not to give?"

"Because," he said, his voice breaking, "if anything should happen to you, I couldn't live with myself."

She looked at him, and he saw the future in her eyes. It promised more heaven than he knew existed, if only they could find their way through the present. "You've never been a fearful man, Sebastian," she said. "Don't fail me now when I need your courage to help get me through this."

He clamped down on the moan rising in his throat but could do nothing to stem the tears suddenly clouding his eyes. Her face grew indistinct, blurred, so that all he had to guide him was the memory of how she looked. Of the way her mouth turned up in a smile; of how her eyes grew drowsy with passion, and her skin flushed with anticipation when he made love to her.

If he were to lose her, this is how it would be: memories growing dimmer each year until all he had left was the fading echo of her voice.

Blindly he reached for her and buried his face against her hair. He'd fought her when he could have been loving her and he was fighting her still because he *did* love her. More than anyone, even Nat.

"You've accused me of not accepting you into this family," he said, when at last he had himself in control again, "and you were right. I didn't want to see you in that light because family members aren't supposed to fall in love. They aren't supposed to *make* love."

"Not even when there's no blood connection between them?" She lifted her face to his. "Oh, Sebastian, you're too fine a man to hide behind that kind of subterfuge."

"Fine? Is that why I repeatedly hurt and rejected you, when all you ever asked for was acceptance? Is that why I engaged a stranger to delve into your private life, instead of having the decency to come straight out and ask you to share yourself with me in every way, and not just between the sheets?"

"I didn't say you were perfect," she whispered, her hands skimming over his features with such tenderness that he could have wept. "Just that—"

The phone rang before she could finish and, for a moment, they both froze. An hour before, he'd have shoved her away, turned his back to her while he answered, shut her out in as many ways as he could devise, just to keep uppermost in both their minds who was in control. Now, he anchored her to his side as he reached out with his other arm and lifted the receiver, holding it so they could both hear.

"Sebastian?" His stepfather's voice shook with emotion.

"I'm here, Hugo," he said steadily. "Lily and I both are. Has there been a change? Should we come back to the hospital?"

"No...no...! I—" He stopped briefly, obviously fighting for composure.

Glancing down, Sebastian saw Lily's eyes fill with tears. Hugging her closer, he said, "It's bad news, isn't it? We'll be there as soon as we can."

"No," Hugo said again. "That's why I'm calling—to tell you that the odds at last have swung in Natalie's favor. She's made a remarkable turnaround and is finally responding to treatment. The doctor was just in to speak to us. It's going to take time, but he's very optimistic she'll make a full recovery."

Sebastian dropped his forehead to Lily's and closed his eyes. "Thank God," he breathed.

"Our reaction exactly," Hugo said. "Listen, I know it's late and you must both be exhausted, so I won't keep you on the phone any longer, but I didn't think you'd mind being disturbed for news like this. Give our love to Lily, and both of you get some sleep. I know your mother and I will."

Slowly Sebastian hung up and turned to face Lily again. "You heard all that?"

Her mouth trembled and a tear rolled down her cheek. "Every word."

He wiped at the tear with his thumb. "Think you'll be able to sleep now?"

She shook her head. "Suddenly I'm not tired anymore."

"Me, neither." He drew her toward him until his mouth grazed hers. "You want to do something else?"

The emotion of the moment had built to a crescendo they knew could be satisfied only one way. Smiling shakily, she said, "It depends."

"Oh, really?" He pressed a kiss to each of her eyelids. "On what?"

"On what else you have in mind." Her hands fluttered over him, refined instruments of torture and delight.

Heat shot through him. Curling his hand around the back of her neck, he steered her down the hall toward the bedroom. "You said earlier that we get into trouble when we talk, and you were right. How about I show you, instead?"

Much later, when she'd exhausted him and he wondered if he'd ever be able to rise to the occasion again, she had the nerve to say she was hungry. "Cripes, woman, you're insatiable," he complained.

"I was thinking about those sandwiches you made. It seems a pity to let them go to waste."

He opened one eye. "You want ketchup on yours?"

Her smile flowed over him like melted honey and from the way his body responded, he decided there was still life in the old tiger, after all. "I want you," she said, walking her fingers down his chest. "With or without ketchup."

They finally ate the cold BLT sandwiches for breakfast, and washed them down with champagne and orange juice. "So where do we go from here?" he asked, watching as she loaded the dirty plates into the dishwasher he never bothered to use.

Even though she had her back to him, he saw the way she stiffened at the question and would have laid money on the doubts suddenly chasing through her mind. "I suppose, to the hospital and eventually, when I know Natalie's really out of the woods, I'll go back to the West Coast."

"How about to the altar with me, instead?"

Silence hung in the air for several seconds before she asked incredulously, "Are you offering to marry me?"

"Well, it's a lousy job, I know, but someone has to do it."

Very slowly, she turned to face him. "Well, thank you very much, but no, I don't think so."

He stared at her, dumbfounded. "Why the hell not, Lily?"

"Because you happened to come into my life at a time when I was feeling lonely and abandoned, and needed someone. Hugo has Cynthia and Natalie and, for a while, I had you. But I never really expected it would be for keeps. You're not the permanent kind, Sebastian. You've told me so yourself, more than once."

"A man can change his mind, can't he?"

"Not for the reasons prompting your actions now. I don't want the words *'For guilt, and pain inflicted, I do,'* included in your wedding vows."

"Then perhaps I haven't made myself clear. My asking you to marry me is not driven by a need to atone for my past sins." He cupped her face in his hands and looked deeply into her eyes. "Last night I told you I love you," he said, inching closer until his mouth was caressing hers. "I still love you this morning. I have loved you for weeks and I will go on loving you for the rest of my life."

"This isn't fair," she sighed. "You're not supposed to be able to seduce me like this. Not again…and not so easily. You're hard and mean and undeserving…I've told myself so a hundred times. You have…no right…proving me wrong."

But her protests were all for show. Her body and her lips and the dreamy expression in her eyes told him she no more believed what she was saying than she did that the moon was made of green cheese.

"I know," he said, backing onto the nearest chair and drawing her down on his lap. "I need a good woman to whip me into shape. Think you're up for the job?"

She wriggled out of his hold and put the safety of the work island between him and her. "I'm not sure."

A flicker of nervousness rippled through him. "Jeez, Lily, I've laid my heart on the line. What more do you want? I can give you a good life, the kind you deserve. There's nothing to keep you in Vancouver—no business, and certainly no family. Why can't you just say yes, and put me out my misery?"

"Oh, I don't know." Thoughtfully she folded the dish towel and hung it over the oven door. "Maybe because I'm an old-fashioned kind of woman who wants an old-fashioned kind of proposal from the heart."

"You mean, you want me down on one knee?"

She planted her fists on her sexy little hips and glared at him. "After all the grief you've put me through in the last few months, Sebastian Caine? You bet I do! I want roses and violins and moonlight and promises of happy-ever-after."

"That kind of promise is hard to keep, Lily. Will you settle for me promising to love you as long as we both shall live, and then some?"

She nibbled the corner of her lip consideringly. "If you'll let me do the same for you."

"Oh," he said, striding around the island and reaching for her, "I think I can safely promise you that."

"In that case, yes, I'll marry you, Sebastian," she said, brazenly pulling open his bathrobe and creating mayhem in places no well-brought up young woman would dare to trespass until the ink was dry on the marriage certificate.

"Better make it soon," he muttered unsteadily. "I don't fancy having to tell Hugo he's about to be a grandfather before he becomes a father-in-law."

*   *   *

They were married six weeks later, in an evening ceremony in the middle of November, two days after the first snowfall had turned Stentonbridge into a winter wonderland and one week after Natalie received a clean bill of health from her doctor.

Dozens of candles illuminated the old stone church. Giant white chrysanthemums and dark green ferns adorned the altar and hung from satin ribbons at the end of the pews.

Cynthia wore midnight-blue silk and wept happy tears all over her orchid corsage. Natalie made a delectable maid of honor in cranberry brocade. And Lily came down the aisle on her father's arm, radiant in an exquisite full-length white velvet wedding gown.

"Hey," Sebastian murmured over the dying chords of the organ, as she came to a stop next to him at the altar. "This is your last chance to run."

"I just did," she told him, her smile dazzling. "How else do you think I wound up here? I've finally come home."

The Dysarts

by Catherine George

*A family with a passion for life—
and for love.*

Get to know the Dysarts!
Over the coming months you can share
the dramas and joys, and hopes and dreams
of this wealthy English family, as unexpected
passions, births and marriages unfold
in their lives.

LORENZO'S REWARD
Harlequin Presents® #2203
on sale September 2001

RESTLESS NIGHTS
Harlequin Presents® #2244
on sale April 2002

Available wherever Harlequin books are sold.

HARLEQUIN®
Makes any time special ®

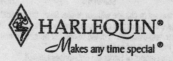

If you enjoyed what you just read,
then we've got an offer you can't resist!

Take 2 bestselling
love stories FREE!
Plus get a FREE surprise gift!

Clip this page and mail it to Harlequin Reader Service®

IN U.S.A.	IN CANADA
3010 Walden Ave.	P.O. Box 609
P.O. Box 1867	Fort Erie, Ontario
Buffalo, N.Y. 14240-1867	L2A 5X3

YES! Please send me 2 free Harlequin Presents® novels and my free surprise gift. After receiving them, if I don't wish to receive anymore, I can return the shipping statement marked cancel. If I don't cancel, I will receive 6 brand-new novels every month, before they're available in stores! In the U.S.A., bill me at the bargain price of $3.34 plus 25¢ shipping & handling per book and applicable sales tax, if any*. In Canada, bill me at the bargain price of $3.74 plus 25¢ shipping & handling per book and applicable taxes**. That's the complete price and a savings of at least 10% off the cover prices—what a great deal! I understand that accepting the 2 free books and gift places me under no obligation ever to buy any books. I can always return a shipment and cancel at any time. Even if I never buy another book from Harlequin, the 2 free books and gift are mine to keep forever.

106 HEN DFNY
306 HEN DC7T

Name	(PLEASE PRINT)	
Address	Apt.#	
City	State/Prov.	Zip/Postal Code

* Terms and prices subject to change without notice. Sales tax applicable in N.Y.
** Canadian residents will be charged applicable provincial taxes and GST.
  All orders subject to approval. Offer limited to one per household and not valid to
  current Harlequin Presents® subscribers..
  ® are registered trademarks of Harlequin Enterprises Limited.

PRES01   ©2001 Harlequin Enterprises Limited